GETTING EVEN

A novel for young adults

PAUL KROPP

AN ARCHWAY PAPERBACK
Published by POCKET BOOKS • NEW YORK

This novel is a work of fiction. Names, characters, places, and incidents are either the product of the author's imagination or are used fictitiously. Any resemblance to actual events or locales or persons, living or dead, is entirely coincidental.

AN ARCHWAY PAPERBACK *Original*

An Archway Paperback published by
POCKET BOOKS, a division of Simon & Schuster, Inc.
1230 Avenue of the Americas, New York, N.Y. 10020

ISBN: 0-671-62419-9

First Archway Paperback printing July, 1986

10 9 8 7 6 5 4 3 2 1

Printed in the U.S.A.

to Sandra Gulland

GETTING EVEN

Chapter 1

KEITH

THE FIRST TIME I SAW JANE, ALL I COULD MAKE OUT was a fuzzy ball of pink sweater topped by a shining mass of blond hair. Jane was on one side of the frosted glass which separates Uncle John's inner sanctum from the rest of the guidance office. I was on the other side, trying to peer through the glass. It seemed to me that the frosted glass made Uncle John's office look like a steamed-up shower stall.

The blue referral slip in my hand meant that the next shower was mine. It was time for another of Uncle John's inspiring talks on living up to my potential. This potential has never seemed very great to me, but Uncle John made a point once each semester of suggesting, not only that I wasn't living up to it, but that I wasn't even in its reasonable vicinity. Uncle John, unfortunately, sets my potential at about the same level as my brother's actual achievement. My brother had once stood over Wagnalls High School in about the same way as Colossus stood over the harbor at Rhodes. Uncle John called me down twice a year to find out why I had yet to become another of the seven wonders of the world.

Obviously I was dreading the interview. As far as I was concerned, the fuzzy shape now talking to Uncle John could keep chatting with him forever, or until the end of my math class, which feels like the same length of time. I could keep busy by staring at my feet, the one part of me that really is colossal.

"Hey, Keith," I heard as the door to the hall flew open. It was Frank Pescatore.

"What are you doing here?" I asked him.

"Got an appointment," he said, grinning his gap-toothed grin. "I gotta talk to Uncle John about college."

"You couldn't get into barber's college," I said.

"Who cares? This blue slip gets me out of Morris' class. She's giving a test on *Macbeth* and I can't keep all those Mac guys straight in my head."

"Did you read it?"

"Nah. Saw the movie. All I remember is these witches didn't have no clothes. And there was this part where some broad is rubbing blood off her hands."

"The sleepwalking scene."

"Yeah. She was *all right*."

These last two words were delivered with a drool which cannot be conveyed in print. In fact, a good deal of Frank's life seems to defy the written word. I remember that he spent the better half of grade six exiled to the hall, but when Mrs. Simpson came to write out the report cards she could find nothing worse to say than "immature." She might have added that Frank was so stupid he had a hard time finding his way out of the cloakroom. Or that he had spent most of that sixth grade trying to trap Marci MacGuire in the cloakroom with him. Teachers tend to ignore what's really important.

"Who's the broad with Uncle John?" he asked.

"I don't know," I said. The girl looked like an unfocused image in the viewfinder of my camera.

"She looks pretty nice to me," Frank said.

"You can't see anything, Frank."

"Oh yeah, you can. You can see the shape of her bod. Just give it a try."

I tried to focus through the distorting glass, but what I came up with was mostly inspired by an overactive imagination. All I could tell for sure was that the girl was blonde and . . . well, big. I shrugged and went back to looking at my shoes.

Frank wasn't as easily discouraged. He reached forward and took hold of the doorhandle.

"What are you doing?" I whispered.

"I'm going to open the door a crack," Frank told me, his own voice hushed.

"Why?"

"To listen, stupid. Besides, I want a better look at the broad in there. I bet she's somebody new."

Frank turned the handle and the door opened, just a crack, as he had predicted. Frank was quiet, listening to what was going on inside.

We could hear Uncle John trying to convince the girl that she'd really enjoy a grade eleven math course. The girl was saying, like any person in his or her right mind, that math was hard, boring, and useless. Neither of them seemed to be aware that the office door had opened.

Frank shot me a look of disappointment as he listened in. I think he expected to overhear some kind of private, intimate conversation. Instead he got the voice of Uncle John droning on about "developing skills for the future."

Frustrated, Frank got up noiselessly from his chair and moved directly across from the doorway. His eyes grew wide. Not only had he seen something, but he liked what he saw.

"What is it?" I whispered.

Frank mouthed a "Wow" and waved for me to come over.

Looking back, I realize that a gentleman would not have gone over to peer into the office. I realize that a gentleman would have closed the door, or coughed, or said "ahem" so as to end this silly game of peeping Tom. A gentleman would have done that and then busied himself with rereading Baudelaire or dusting a bit of caviar off his tie or studying the catalogue from Princeton. My brother was once that kind of gentleman.

I, however, am not.

Maybe just to prove that point, I snuck over beside Frank and craned my neck to see the girl inside. What I saw was Jane, or, to be precise, a certain part of Jane.

"Look at those boobs," Frank whispered.

That's exactly what I was doing. Our position outside the door, the size of the door opening, and the angle thus formed—you might say, mathematically—put a limit on the field of view.

Unfortunately, Frank's whisper had been a little too loud. The next thing we knew, the girl inside leaned forward and stared right at the two of us. The expression on her face told the whole story. If she had been holding a can of Raid, we'd have been two very dead bugs.

I blushed. I tried to pretend that my focus had actually been on the bulletin board behind her head, but this effort did nothing to fool her. The office door slammed with a bang.

"We're in trouble now," I told Frank.

"Who cares?" Frank said, as relaxed as I was embarrassed. "It's no crime to give 'em the old eyeball. You gotta get a little confidence, Keith, a little . . . as the French say, savvy vous."

"You mean *savoir faire*, Frank. Would you spare me the lecture? I don't need your advice before I get another load of it from Uncle John."

"What you need—" Frank began, but his words stopped when the door to Uncle John's office opened wide. The girl we had ogled stepped out of the office. She had a forced smile on her face as she thanked Uncle John and carefully closed his office door. Then she turned on the two of us.

"Why don't you two . . ."

I won't report the rest of what Jane said, but its effect was strong enough to make even Frank turn somewhat red from embarrassment. As for me, well, you could have fried an egg on each of my cheeks.

Chapter 2

JANE

"WHY DON'T YOU TWO F— RIGHT OFF!" IS WHAT I said.

It's typical of Keith that he won't report openly just what I said, as if the offending word were too, too much even when abbreviated. Personally, I wonder why I should bother with abbreviation. A ten-minute walk around the average high school will show you a lot more f-words written on walls or scratched into desks than I could use in a lifetime.

It's also typical of Keith that *he* should be embarrassed when *I* swear or when Frank acts like an animal, two fairly regular occurrences. This is all part of a very elaborate problem of his having to do with a dominant superego and a relatively weak self-image. Since all that may sound rather technical, why don't I just sum it up by saying that Keith is the kind of person who always cuts the crusts off his sandwiches.

Now you can see why Keith's version of this story will be more subdued than mine. *I* know that all the flavor is in the crusts.

My first impression of Keith? A Piggie, pure and simple, pink and porcine. A Piggie, for those of you stranded in some other century, is any guy whose real goal in life is to be able to write one nonimaginary letter-to-the-editor of *Penthouse*. Most guys in high school are Piggies and Keith gave me no reason to think he was different from the rest. There, outside Goodie's office, were two strange-looking guys whose *entire* attention was focused between my neck and my waist.

Keith and Frank were a fine opening to my first day at Wagnalls—the only public school I've ever attended and the only school I've ever heard of named after half a dictionary. My first thought when I walked into the place was to wonder if the other high school in town was named after Funk.

But I'm getting off topic. Keith frequently tells me that I'm not very organized, which is true, but the only reason he mentions it is that he is obsessively organized. Keith worries if his English essays aren't finished a *week* before the due date. Keith never had to do anything on locker clean-out days because his locker is *already* spotless. Keith, in short, verges on being mentally ill.

I, on the other hand, do not stop at verging.

But Keith says the idea of this book is to tell a story and if you're going to tell a story then you're supposed to start at the beginning. Right? So we might as well start with my personal beginning on day one, sixteen years before I showed my face at Wagnalls. My birth itself was ignored by almost everyone except my mother, who didn't have too much choice in the matter, because my father had just landed a new announcing job in New York City. Shortly after the congratulations for him died down, we left Ohio and settled in the only city in the world proud to be nicknamed after a large fruit.

My father did well in New York and was quickly dubbed the Golden Voice of Radio as part of the usual station hype. That description is actually quite accurate—or at least it used to be. His voice was so smooth and so low that it made the average newscaster sound like a squeaky transvestite.

As my father moved from news to talk shows to "personality" status, I went from booties to Buster Browns to Adidas runners. The two of us thrived. My mother did not. I would daily trudge off to private school; my father would grab a taxi to the station; my mother would visit her analyst. She was trying to "get well." At some point it became pretty clear that my mother would never, ever get well. She underlined this point by abruptly leaving both my father and me, disappearing from the face of the earth for all we knew.

I was twelve. My father was at the peak of his career. And my mother had cut herself off from us. That's when I started dreaming about her. Nightmares at first, then strange dreams with her face, closed doors, and empty spaces—dreams like demented rock videos.

That's also when the trouble between my father and me got started. Now the analysts may say that this is related to transference of guilt or a reversed Oedipal complex, but all that is a bit much. I prefer to think that I loathed my father for his deficiencies rather than for mine. After all, I wasn't the one making out with the receptionist in Studio B when my mother dropped by to visit.

Anyway, my father's career went into a slide after my mother left. He was bounced down when his station changed formats, then moved to a middle-of-the-road FM slot. He was close to the axe there when we moved to Toronto so Golden Voice could make a fresh start as an ordinary news reader. This was a little too mundane after his previous star status, so when he got a decent offer in this tiny burg, he took it. I couldn't blame him, could I? You bet I could! The idea of moving out to the boonies seemed as attractive as a prefrontal lobotomy without anesthetic. And I figured the effects would be the same.

We moved at the end of August. My father phoned my mother to tell her. I didn't talk to her. I haven't talked to her since she walked out on us four years ago. And I won't talk to her until, well, until I'm good and ready to. I wrote my mother's obituary years ago in New York. If she thinks she can just come waltzing back into my life when she feels like it, she's dead wrong. She's positively deceased.

Anyway, in September my father took over the microphones at the local 50,000-watt station which beams out over the town and umpteen miles of farmland. I took residence at Wagnalls and spent my first day in a state of shock. Not just from Keith and Frank—but from *everything*. Wagnalls was not only the first public school I'd ever attended, it was in a town where every kid had known every other kid since the womb. And I was supposed to blend in. Fat chance!

When I met Mr. Goodie—I'm not kidding, that's

Uncle John's real name—I knew that I was in the last bastion of mediocrity. If any teacher had dared to dress like that at a private school in New York, the headmistress would have sent him to shovel coal into the boilers. At Wagnalls, however, Uncle John was the sartorial norm: rumpled plaid sports coat, too-wide tie, shiny-bottomed pants, and white patent leather shoes. Can you imagine anybody still wearing an outfit like that? It was bad enough that they had to kill millions of helpless baby polyesters to produce the coat and pants, but white shoes?

My interview with Uncle John seems funny when I look back on it. We were mutually astonished by each other. I couldn't believe that any living human being could spout so many clichés in the course of a twenty-minute conversation. Uncle John, for his part, couldn't believe me. When I told him that I wanted to go to Yale, Vassar, or Barnard, in that order of preference, he gave me a look as if my delusions of grandeur would shortly have me married to Napoleon. I didn't know at the time that only one person in the entire history of Wagnalls H.S. had *ever* been accepted into the Ivy League. And that person happened to be Keith's brother.

I went on to tell Uncle John that I was interested in psychology, though probably not inclined towards the medical training required for a psychiatric degree. Uncle John nodded as if he understood what I was talking about. I admitted that I had been in analysis myself, off and on, and Uncle John nodded again. Then he launched into a lecture on the virtues of taking math, a lecture which had no connection to *anything* I had told him.

It was during the lecture that I noticed four piggish eyes staring at me. I slammed the door on them, wondering if the Piggies had gotten an earful as well as an eyeful, while Uncle John went on urging me to get involved with the school by playing volleyball.

It was easy enough to say yes to that, so I did. My mind wasn't on volleyball at the time, it was on vengeance against those two Piggies. I figured these guys probably couldn't handle a nice, big swearword coming from a nice girl like me with freckles and apple cheeks, so I politely said goodbye to Uncle John and proceeded to let them have it. I just couldn't pass up the chance to get even.

Chapter 3

KEITH

BEFORE WE GET TOO FAR INTO THIS, I'D JUST LIKE TO say for the record that I do not cut the crusts off my sandwiches. Sometimes I think Jane is too ready to sacrifice the truth just so she can get off a clever remark. I would never say that Jane is the kind of person who rips sandwiches in half with her bare hands unless I had personally checked it out and seen the salami go flying.

All of this is just a digression from the story that began in Uncle John's office. As I suspected, Uncle John had called me down to give me the "Why Not Get Involved" speech. I had a hunch that particular talk was coming up since I had already sat through the "What Do You Intend to Do with Your Life" and "You're Not Living Up to Your Potential" speeches in grade ten.

The trick of escaping from Uncle John's "Why Not Get Involved" talk is to go out for a sport or sign up for a club. Unfortunately, I hate sports and despise clubs. I'm just not a joiner. For a moment I thought of explaining to Uncle John that any large group of people—say any crowd of three or more—is dangerously close to becoming a mob and makes me terribly nervous. Or I might have said that I'm allergic to the phoney friendships in clubs and sports, that they make me sneeze.

But I didn't. Uncle John cannot be reasoned with, and I cave in easily when faced with single-minded lunatics. I simply told him that okay, I'd take pictures for the yearbook. As soon as I said it, I cursed my own weakness. But in the long run, it was precisely that moment of cowardice that led me to see more of Jane Flemming than just her, uh, anger.

Three days later, I was sitting at the back of Mrs. Morris's room waiting for the yearbook meeting to start. The staff from the previous year had gathered in front, busy joking with each other, clustering around a tall guy with thick glasses whom I recognized as the editor. I felt somewhat isolated sitting in back, but social assertiveness has never been one of my strong suits. In fact, I was wondering if I had any strong suits when Frank plopped down in the seat next to mine.

"Hey-hey."

I nodded. It occurred to me that Frank was even more out of place at this meeting than I was.

"When's the show gonna start?"

"Don't know."

"That's the trouble with this place, you know. You try to brown-nose a few points and then they waste your time. I'm gonna be late to football practice 'cause of this, and Whyte don't like it when you come in late. Know what I mean?"

I had no idea what he meant, but I nodded anyhow.

"How come you're here, Keith?" he went on. "I mean, you haven't gone out for nothing since softball back in sixth grade, you know?"

"Uncle John hit me with 'Get Involved.' "

"Oh yeah. I never got that one. He keeps getting me with the old 'Maturing' speech. It was my lousy mark in Morris's class that got me here. She said maybe I could be a sportswriter 'cause I couldn't write nothin' else. You gonna write stuff?" Frank asked.

"Pictures," I said quietly.

"What's that?" he asked loudly.

"I'm going to take pictures, I think."

"You know, I got a camera too. An Instamatic, but it takes lousy pictures, all fuzzy at the edges. Maybe I could do a centerfold for the yearbook. Get Jill Hawes or one of the cheerleaders to, you know . . ."

"Sure, Frank."

"Say, was your brother a photog too? I mean, he did everything else, didn't he? Nudge-nudge, wink-wink."

"Yeah, but he didn't take pictures of it," I said.

"You know, you never did tell me the real story about your brother and that library teacher. I've heard a lot of stories and I always kinda wondered what went on. You know?"

"Shhh. They're starting."

Mrs. Morris stomped into the room and closed the heavy door behind her. Lou Russell, the editor, got to his feet and towered over everyone in the room. He must have been six-six in spite of his perpetual stoop. I had seen him loping through the school and it always amazed me that he cultivated that Ichabod Crane look instead of being embarrassed by it. Lou was a senior, of course, and he had joined the yearbook staff back when my brother was the editor. He was one of the few people still at Wagnalls who had an accurate memory of what Steven Hartman did when he was there.

Lou made a list of deadlines on the blackboard while a sheet circulated through the room asking for our names and areas of interest. When it reached me, I penciled "photography" in tiny, neat letters just below where Frank had scrawled "SPORTS." Up in front, Lou had a copy of last year's dummy and some samples of the copy and photographs that had gone off to the printers. By the time he had finished explaining all this, the sign-up sheet had returned to the front of the classroom.

"Oh, great," he said, staring at the list. "I've got a dozen writers, two people besides me who can do layout, and two photographers. That's exactly the opposite of what we need. Can any of you *soi-disant* writers operate a camera?"

"I got an Instamatic," Frank volunteered.

"Great," Lou answered, dismissing him with a look. "Anybody else?"

Everyone was silent. Lou leaned against the blackboard. Mrs. Morris was marking at her desk.

"Okay. Can I see you photographers right now and we'll have a meeting with you writers next week on Thursday after I get the dummy made up."

This was enough to dissolve the group, leaving only Frank, myself, and little Charlie Fisher standing around the front desk.

"Hey, you want me to stay?" Frank asked.

"You're the guy with the Instamatic, right? Let's see—Frank Pescatore."

"That's the name. You want me here? I'm sort of in a hurry."

"Thanks for volunteering, Frank, but I need a sportswriter too. If I get in a tough spot, I'll be in touch. Okay?"

Frank waved and headed off through the door, as oblivious to the brush-off as he was to everything else. I envied him. There's a lot to be said for brashness or stupidity or whatever it is that lets people like Frank get on so easily in the world.

"So you're Keith Hartman. I used to know your brother."

I nodded. It occurred to me that Steven's spirit was everywhere. I don't call him "god" for nothing.

Lou turned to the short kid standing beside me. "It's good to have you back, Charlie. I know that you've got your dad's darkroom. But what about you, Keith?"

"I, uh, can do my own black and white."

"And what do you shoot with?"

"I've been using the Nikon lately," Charlie announced, "but I might be able to get hold of the Hasselblad for club shots."

I think I coughed out something about my Olympus at that point, feeling hopelessly outclassed.

"Look, we've got to get going on the team shots right away. Did either of you bring a camera?" Lou asked.

"How about tomorrow?" Charlie replied.

"No, I've got Jennings and the volleyball girls all set. What about you, Keith?"

"I guess I could." I had brought my camera to school, intending to take some pictures on the way home. I had not, I repeat, *not* intended to take any pictures of the girls' volleyball team.

"Looks like it's you, Keith. It's all arranged with Mrs. Jennings. They'll be expecting you down in the big gym."

He walked over to the file cabinet behind Mrs. Morris's desk as if the matter were fully explained. I didn't move. I was paralyzed. He actually expected me to walk into a girls' volleyball practice and start taking pictures.

I considered the possibility of following Charlie Fisher and simply walking right out of the room. Except I would walk out forever. I'd sign up for the chess club instead. I'd join the tiddlywinks team. I'd do something—anything—but I wouldn't go down to the gym.

"Hey, wait a minute," Lou called as I edged toward the door. "You don't even know what you're doing yet."

I couldn't have agreed more.

"Here," Lou said, returning from the file cabinet with a piece of paper in his hand. "This should help. It's a dummy of the volleyball spread. We're going to need the big team shot up here and probably one good action shot down here. Don't give me something with five hundred players for this tiny space. I need one snappy action shot of one or two of the girls. Use the good-looking ones, it never hurts," he said, dropping his voice so Mrs. Morris wouldn't hear.

"I guess so." There must have been panic in my voice.

"What's the matter? Are you embarrassed about doing a girls' team?"

"Sort of," I admitted. Actually, it was beyond embarrassment, it was raw fear.

"Keith, it's like anything else. The first time is the hardest. If you're nervous about starting off, try making up a little script before you go down to the gym."

"Like what?"

"Something like, 'Mrs. Jennings, I'm Keith Hartman, the yearbook photographer. I'd like to take some pictures during practice today.' There you go. Just practice the lines and you'll be all set for the job."

"I'm . . . uh . . . Keith Jennings, the . . . Oh, I blew it."

"Try it again."

"I'm Keith Hartman. I'm the yearbook photographer and I want to take some pictures . . . during practice today."

"Perfect," Lou said, his face beaming confidence. "Don't forget to make an appointment for the group shot. And, oh yeah, we'll reimburse you for the film. Now go to it. We're counting on you." He patted me on the back as he led me to the door.

It wasn't until I reached the end of the hall that the full horror of the idea got to me. It hit me in my stomach, which responded with such growling and churning that I'm certain my navel was vibrating under my sweater. Still, there was nothing to do but go ahead.

Chapter 4

JANE

I DIDN'T *SEE* KEITH COME INTO THE GYM, BUT I *heard* Nancy Suddaby yell out his presence in a voice loud enough to make the bleachers rattle. The squad turned to see what species of male flesh was going to record them for posterity, then emitted a collective sigh because it was only Keith.

The rest of them began giggling and primping anyway, as if they were posing for *Seventeen* fashion layouts. Gracie Ratinski was the worst of these, rushing off to the change room for more lipstick and eyeliner, though her face already looked like it was painted on with crayons.

I didn't join in all this effort just for a sixteenth-inch picture in the school yearbook. For one thing, I think nobody's more ridiculous than when they're trying to make themselves look good. For another thing, I regarded the total intelligence of the volleyball squad as just this side of trainable retarded. No way I was going to start acting like the rest of them.

Besides, I recognized Keith as one of the two Piggies from the guidance office. I asked Patty Something-or-other what his name was. She went into a long explanation about Keith and his brother that told me a lot more than his name. I knew that this was my chance. Never get mad, Jane says. Get even.

Keith was busy staring at his shoes when Mrs. Jennings went over to him. "You must be the yearbook photographer for the team pictures," she said, trying to lift his attention from his toes.

"I'm Keith Hartman, the . . . uh . . . yearbook photographer, and I'd like to take some pictures." Keith uttered his line with a voice that sounded like it came from a home computer. A couple of girls laughed. Mrs. J. looked at him in a funny way.

"Right," she said. "Do you want the girls to pose or will these be candid shots?"

"Uh, candids, I guess."

"Good luck. We've got another half hour, if that's time enough for you."

"Oh, plenty," Keith said.

We got back to playing volleyball while Keith went over to the bleachers and began playing with his camera. Well, that's what it looked like. He spent ten minutes screwing lenses and trying to put film in and setting off the flash while it was pointed at his face.

Keith *finally* managed to get his equipment together and muster up enough courage to come closer to where we were practicing. He was using a big telephoto lens, as if he were expecting to shoot photos of charging rhinoceri from the safety of a hilltop two miles away. I couldn't blame him for that. If I had to take a picture of Nancy Suddaby, I'd probably want to use a telescope just to keep my distance.

Keith spent a good five minutes staring through the viewfinder. I began to think he had his eyeball stuck to the camera. When, at last, he took a picture, it cleverly caught the back of everybody's head.

Mrs. J. called for a scrimmage between the two squads, probably because Keith's efforts were so pathetic that she wanted to do something—*anything*—to improve the yearbook shots. I served the ball nice and easy so we could get a volley started. Gracie Ratinski hit it back, her bright red smile glowing at us from across the net. Margie Saltzman was at net and went up to smash the ball, all two hundred pounds of her ready to kill. Keith's flash went off. Blinded by the light, Margie missed the ball entirely and fell flat on the floor with all the grace of a hippopotamus doing a plié. Talk about gross.

Two other girls in the front line blinked away the spots and complained to Mrs. J. I watched as Keith moved closer to the net, maybe trying to get one of those artsy through-the-net shots which became passé ten years ago. He kept moving forward with his eye glued to the camera. In front of him was a wooden chair with a back just high enough to hit Keith right where it hurts. I could see the collision coming . . .

Grunt.

The chair toppled over and Keith reached down to grab at the source of the pain. Then he remembered where he was, yanked his hands away, and turned a bright apple red.

The squad went crazy. Keith suffered more hooting and hollering than the male strippers I saw once in Toronto. He probably wondered if his school insurance paid anything for death by embarrassment.

Mrs. J. moved in to rescue him. "Maybe it would work better if you posed the pictures."

"Huh?" he said.

"We've got to pack up the practice now, but I could ask a few girls to stay behind and pose for you. That might be easier," she said.

"Oh, yeah."

"Fine," she told him, turning around to us. "Okay, girls, photo session. We need some volunteers to get in the yearbook pictures. Don't inundate me with a sea of hands, three or four of you will do."

For a minute, there were no hands at all. I thought this was pretty amazing, given the vanity usually shown by the girls on the team. There was a lot of giggling and a lot of you-do-its passed among the group, but no hands.

"Come on, stars. We need somebody to start us off," Mrs. J. prompted.

The team giggled again, for no apparent reason. That is, the rest of the team giggled. I *do not* giggle; I laugh. But at this point, I wasn't laughing. I was still thinking about revenge.

"Nancy says she'll do it," I shouted out. I figured that Nancy Suddaby would be a little more than our bumbling photographer could handle.

"Only if Jane does it too," Nancy shot back, showing a little more cleverness than I had expected.

After the two of us had roped each other into the project, everybody else wanted to join in. Eventually Mrs. J. picked Shelley, Gloria, and Patty to fill out the group.

The rest of the squad headed off to the change room, not without comments about the five of us staying back. We stood around the net waiting for Keith to say something. Eventually he did.

"Uh, could two of you sort of jump up for the ball?"

Gloria Durney immediately volunteered and forced Patty Something-or-other to join her. The two of them jumped up while Keith squatted by the net and pressed the shutter release. But the flash didn't fire.

Keith was perplexed.

"What's that buzzing noise?" I asked.

"It's the flash recharging," Keith said.

"Oh. I thought it was your teeth chattering."

That got a laugh from Patty Something-or-other and a smile from the others. Not bad for starters, I thought. I kept on giving Keith my liquid-nitrogen stare.

"Come on, Jane. You get in the picture," Nancy suggested.

"This is the last shot," Keith announced.

"All right," I said, archly enough. "Ansel Adams you're not, but I guess you'll have to do."

Keith asked me to jump up and tap at a ball that Gloria would set up for me. I thought the whole idea was pretty boring, but it was only after Keith had snapped the shutter that the real dangers came crawling home to me. I mean, I take a cruddy picture at the best of times. My freckles show too much or my cheeks look like pumpkins or my body just comes out too fat. Basically, I don't like my freckles, my face, or my body, and pictures just serve to remind me of all this. Suddenly I was afraid that Keith's picture would make me look *awful*.

"Hey," I said to Keith, "I just want you to know—

you can't use any picture of me unless I give the okay. Or I'll sue."

"What?"

"You didn't get any model release from me," I explained. "So you don't have any right to use that picture."

Keith looked clueless.

"So check with me first," I told him.

"Okay, okay."

I turned my back on him and walked off towards the locker room. I had a hunch that his piggish eyes were fixed on my rear end and that made me angry.

"By the way," he called out, "how did you ever hear about Ansel Adams?"

"I *read*. You should try it sometime," I said. "Or maybe your brother has a monopoly on brains in the family, huh?"

The last line just cut Keith dead. The onset of rigor mortis was so obvious that even I felt bad. All the color drained from Keith's face and he just stood there with his mouth open.

How was I supposed to know that my last shot would hit just where Keith's armor was weakest? I didn't want to destroy the guy—I just wanted to get even.

What's so rotten about that?

Chapter 5

KEITH

"A MONOPOLY ON BRAINS." A SHOT LIKE THAT WAS just what I needed. After Jane's parting words, to say that I slunk home would be an exaggeration. I didn't have enough pride left to slink.

I made it to my room and opened *Lord of the Rings*. I tried to resume a third rereading, but my mind wasn't on it. My eyes moved across the page but the magic wasn't there. I kept thinking back to school, to the gym, to Jane Flemming, and to my brother's supposed monopoly on brains.

"Keith!"

I was lying on my bed, picturing Jane's face, wondering whether I hated her or merely despised her. Jane has a baby face, and that makes her nastiness harder to take. The freckles and the big cheeks give her a certain look of innocence, so when someone like that makes you feel miserable, it comes as a real surprise.

"Keith, it's time for dinner," my mother bellowed.

I shut the Tolkien with a sigh, rolled out of bed, and walked down to the kitchen. In Middle Earth, Gandalf was seeking the first ring of power while the forces of Mordred assembled to destroy Dale and the land of the Hobbits. In the kitchen, my mother would once again be serving up scrambled eggs on toast.

"Keith, tell your father it's time to eat," my mother ordered.

She was crashing around, looking absurd in a conservative brown suit with a frilly pink apron tied on to protect it. I watched her flying between the counter and the stove, amazed as always at the fury with which she attacks the preparation of dinner. My mother becomes a madwoman when putting a meal together, as if getting the job done faster will make the food better. I watched as she flung scrambled eggs onto toast with such speed that a fair portion of the mess landed on the Formica.

"Don't just stand there. I've got a meeting at seven and can't dillydally over dinner."

Since her manic cooking was making me nervous anyway, I left the kitchen and went down to the rec room. My father was down there playing a Bach Passacaglia and Fugue on the organ with his usual mechanical precision. I waited for the music to reach a cadence so I could shout the discouraging news of dinner. But when he had introduced the fugue subject for the third time, I figured I had better just break into the middle of things.

"Dad," I yelled. There was no immediate effect beyond some fingering problems at the keyboard. "We've got to eat."

"Uh-huh," my father said, going right ahead with the piece.

There didn't seem to be much more I could do about that, short of unplugging the air compressor for the organ, so I walked back upstairs.

"Where's your father?" my mother asked, as if the continuing organ notes provided no answer. I'm always amazed at the way in which parents fail to grasp the most obvious information.

"Coming."

"Well, his dinner will be cold if he doesn't hurry up."

I nodded and cut into the scrambled eggs with a fork. They needed salt. And pepper.

My mother may bear some physical resemblance to Julia Child, but there the resemblance ends. Not that she cares. In a previous incarnation, she frequently told us, she had servants to take care of trivia like cooking and cleaning. In her current incarnation, alas, the budget couldn't quite handle servants.

My father had once tried to learn how to cook himself, but the results were mediocre. He would have preferred his recipes in cc's and milligrams, his hollandaise sauce made in beakers and flasks, and an oven accurate to a tenth of a degree. As a result, the art of cooking was lost on him. And my mother never even dignified cooking with the word art.

"Sorry for the delay," my dad said, arriving at last.

"Your eggs will be cold by now."

"Sorry."

"Well, Keith," my mother said, turning to me, "how was your day at school?"

Dinner had begun. Some families begin their meals with a prayer, some just dive silently into their food. At our house, dinner starts with a question: "How was your day?" Steven used to answer this in some detail, usually filling in the time between salad and dessert. I tend to say less.

"The pits," I said.

"That's too bad," my mother offered in sympathy. "I had a rotten day too—on the phone all afternoon talking to Esther about this candidate search committee meeting tonight. She told me, though of course I don't know this officially yet, but she said that there are three names coming forward tonight. One of them is this Pescatore fellow who dropped a truckload of garbage in front of city hall. Can you imagine that? And now he wants to run for mayor. Well, I told her, 'Over my dead body,' is what I told her. We may be desperate for a candidate but we'll never be *that* desperate. Besides the garbage thing, I hear that his politics are slightly to the right of Joseph Goebbels."

"Who's he?" I ventured.

"Hitler's propaganda chief," my father said. This brief question and answer caused not even a pause in my mother's monologue.

"You know who's behind it? Steven warned me when I appointed Dr. Suddaby to the committee that the man was going to cause trouble. Now Esther says that he railroaded Pescatore onto the final list and did all the contact work himself. It's almost as if the whole thing was a setup. And unless I put the kibosh on the whole plan, he'll go right through and get nominated. Can you beat that?"

My mother's question was greeted with silence. My dad and I both thought it was merely rhetorical.

"Don't you have any opinion?" she asked, staring now at my father. "You want to see Pescatore as the mayor?"

"I think it's terrible," he answered. Her question seemed to draw him back from some other line of thought.

"Terrible," I echoed. Actually, the idea of Frank's father becoming the mayor struck me as pretty funny.

"You know, that's the trouble around here, that you two don't get involved in these things. Politics are important, not just for us but for a lot of little people out there who are dependent on what the government does. We can sit back with our middle-class complacency knowing that we're pretty well taken care of while this town goes down the drain." My mother had used almost the same words when she was guest speaker in my history class last year. "I haven't had a good political discussion around here since Steven went off to Ann Arbor."

"I'm sorry, dear . . ." my father began. I could tell that he was going to begin his third apology of the night and I had to stop him short. I couldn't take it.

I tossed my fork on the plate so it made a clatter, then stood up. The two of them stared at me, but I didn't care any more. I was sick of hearing about Steven, sick of my mother and her politics, sick of everything. I stormed away from the table, trying to hold everything inside, but I couldn't stop the tears when I finally reached my room.

Downstairs I heard my parents in some kind of

discussion, probably about me. I picked up *Lord of the Rings* again, but my eyes wouldn't focus. I heard the front door open and close. My mother had gone out. A minute later the car started up in the driveway and she was off. Somehow that made me feel better, calmer. I lay back on my bed and tried to think about something, anything, but my mind was still a jumble.

I heard my father come up the stairs. There was a moment's hesitation before he knocked on my door.

"Keith?"

"Yeah."

"Can I come in?"

"If you want," I said.

He came into my room, saw where I was sprawled on the bed, and then sat down on the only chair. My room seemed small with the two of us in it.

"Bad day?" he began.

"Yeah. And I'm still hungry."

"So am I," he admitted. "I'll go out for some Big Macs later. Will that make you feel better?"

"Yeah," I said. "I'd like that."

"Your mother is sorry she got you upset," he explained.

"It wasn't just her."

"Well, sometimes it is. I don't think she sees the differences between you and Steven. I don't know if she ever will."

I looked up and focused on my father's face for the first time in months. It's funny how we don't pay attention to the people we live with, assuming that they never change, that the image we carry from last year or five years ago will always be true. I noticed that my father had more wrinkles than I remembered, especially around the eyes. My father caught me looking at him. I felt embarrassed and so did he.

"What happened at school?" he asked, changing the subject.

"I signed up for the yearbook, to take pictures."

"When do you start?"

"I already did. That's part of the problem," I admitted.

"The yearbook used to drive Steven crazy too," my father said.

"Yeah, but he was the editor."

"That doesn't mean his problems were any more important than yours, just different. Why don't you set up the darkroom and see how your pictures came out?" he suggested.

"Are you going to be downstairs?"

"No, I have to write out the bills."

"Okay, then. I'll set up."

There was no sensible reason why I couldn't have done the darkroom work in one corner of the basement while my father played the organ. But sensible reasons don't have much to do with family life. My father had a sense of space that made other people, me included, feel awkward. It was as if he had drawn a twenty-foot circle around himself. Other people could sometimes come inside the circle, but not for long, and not very comfortably. Often I felt like that, too. I remember my father once said that I was too much like him. I asked him if that was such a bad thing and he just laughed. Maybe he didn't know either.

With my father upstairs, I had the basement to

myself. I set up everything over the old laundry tubs, then loaded the film onto the stainless steel reel. I mixed the developer and adjusted its temperature before I poured it into the tank. Then I had time to think. And worry. Maybe light had fogged the film or the shutter had failed or the flash synch had malfunctioned. Maybe I had knocked the lens out of register or broken the shutter. Maybe all of the girls would look awful and they'd hate me forever. . . . In the next twenty minutes every conceivable problem went through my head. I couldn't relax until I pulled the finished negs off the reel and hung them up to dry.

When I went upstairs, my father looked up from his desk. "How'd they come out?" he asked me.

But I didn't have to answer him out loud. The smile on my face said everything.

Chapter 6

JANE

ALL RIGHT, KEITH, I'M SORRY. I MEAN IT—*I'M sorry*. There, I've said it twice—once in italics—so it must be official. You see, I had Keith pegged as a Piggie, an *oink* of the human variety. I didn't realize at the time that his ego would barely fill the bottom of a thimble. And I didn't know, then, that the image of his brother was half his problem.

Also, I was wrong when I categorized Keith as a Piggie. I realize that now. Technically, Keith is an Iggie, something of an ignoramus when it comes to girls and sex. He's the kind of guy who'll listen to a dirty joke but have to have it explained to him before he can get it. No offense, Keith. A lot of guys are *worse*, as I found out. But all that comes later in the story and we're not there yet.

By mid-October I was no longer a novelty at the school, but I still didn't "fit in," as Uncle John would say. It was obvious to me that I would never *fit in*. It was also obvious that I didn't really want to.

Wagnalls was dominated by Yahoos. A Yahoo, of course, is Jonathan Swift's word for a species of humans who have "a strange disposition for nastiness and dirt." I did an oral book report in English on this, thinking all the time that Swift was describing a good ninety percent of the inhabitants of the class in front of me. Good old Funk 'n' Wagnalls—the Yahoos even slur the name of their school for the lousy little laugh they can get from that.

Personally, I have gone to a number of schools where, if your father were only a neurosurgeon, you might be eligible for a Care package at Christmas. At Wagnalls the Yahoos dressed as if their clothes had *come* from a Care package.

So at Wagnalls they called me a snob. Did I care? Did the girl with her nose in the air and the two-by-four chip on her shoulder give a second thought to anything the Yahoos thought?

Not so that anybody would notice.

Except maybe my father.

"Stick with it, Jane," said the Golden Voice.

I complained to him a lot, not that there was any particular response. I think that could be the whole problem with radio announcers. They're tested to make sure they never get flustered on the air. It doesn't matter if Daffy Duck comes walking into the studio and tries to hustle the receptionist, still the news drones on. Always the golden voice, the mechanical inflections, the splendid and undisturbed basso profundo. It's enough to make a real human sick. Sometimes when I talk to my father I feel like I'm some loony calling up his talk show. He just humors me, twisting around what I say until I end up sounding like some flea brain.

Is that why I hated him?

No, it's only *one* of the reasons why I hated him.

But all this is confusing and not part of the story. The story goes back to Wagnalls and that collection of misfits and lost souls they call teachers.

My days from nine to three were dominated by three miserable excuses for humanity and one outstanding teacher. Let me deal first with the three baddies. *One:* Mrs. Morris, English. Her idea of a legitimate response to *Moby Dick* is to carve a soapstone whale. When I tried to bring up Freudian phallic symbols in class, she sent me to the hall. When I suggested that she was only showing her own sexual frustrations by punishing me, she sent me to the office. I do not get along with Mrs. Morris. I will *never* get along with Mrs. Morris. *Two:* Mr. Weasel, Math. I do not like math. It seems to me that the calculator and the charge card have made mathematics obsolete. So there. *Three:* Mr. Shank, History. A sexist pig. Shank believes that the deciding point in history was when Columbus returned to Spain with VD. Whom does he blame? Not Columbus.

There was one outstanding person at Wagnalls: her name is Mrs. Jennings and her official function at the school is to teach Phys. Ed. Her real function at the school has to do with repairing the damage that the world outside frequently does to its kids.

She was someone I could talk to. The fact that Mrs. Jennings is the volleyball coach probably had a lot to do with my staying on the team. Otherwise I would never have been down in the gym when Keith reappeared to take the volleyball group photo.

I had a hunch he was coming even before those two huge feet of his actually brought him into the gym. The other kids had gone into practice wearing all sorts of makeup, as if their infinitesimal faces in the group photo would somehow look better with heavy mascara.

When Keith came in, I admit I felt a little guilty about the way I had treated him. Whenever I had passed him in the halls, Keith didn't just avert his eyes, he averted his *toes*. So I knew, even then, that I had stuck it to him a little too hard. But he had deserved it, hadn't he?

I knew Keith was still upset about it because he paid absolutely no attention to me as he set up for the shot. In fact, he was so busy paying no attention to me that I *knew* he was paying attention to me. So naturally I paid no attention to him.

Mrs. J. talked to Keith for a minute while I practiced setting up for Marianne's spike. Then Mrs. J. blew her whistle and ordered us to line up by the net. There followed a period of confusion while everyone offered different suggestions about where the lines would go, who would be first, and what order it would all follow. It was obvious to me that the fifteen of us left on the team would make a pretty boring shot if we were just lined up against a wall. Apparently that was obvious to Keith as well. He asked us to gather around in a semicircle, all of us reaching out at a volleyball held up by Nancy Suddaby. Keith got up on a chair to see what this configuration looked like.

"Uh, could we fix the heights a little?" he said,

waving his hand as if that might mean something. "Maybe you two girls could go down there . . . and Nancy and, uh, Jane, you move in."

So he knew my name. Of course, it was a small school, so I imagine everybody knew my name. Jane Flemming, the one who said old bag Morris is sexually frustrated, the one who said Shank is a pervert. Yeah, they all knew me.

Still, I was surprised that Keith had the guts to talk to me, much less give an order. He seemed a little more assured than the week before, and, surprisingly enough, he even had begun to look a little better—if you like the small-town type.

"Mrs. Jennings, could you move in a bit, please?"

She did and the flash went off in our collective faces.

"Hey, you didn't give us any warning! Aren't we supposed to say cheese or something?" Nancy Suddaby shouted at him.

Mrs. J. did the answering. "That's fine, Nancy. *You* say cheese and all the rest of us will just smile . . ."

That got everybody laughing except, of course, Nancy Suddaby. Keith's flash caught us this second time with natural smiles. The whole photographic thing continued for another ten minutes, with Mrs. J. joking around to keep us happy, Keith moving himself and his chair around to take the shots, and the rest of us seeing red and green spots after the flash went off. I had to give Keith some credit. The usual yearbook photograph has you standing awkwardly in front of an auditorium curtain. Keith's team picture would at least be different.

While we were going through all this, I became curious about the pictures he had taken the week before. Maybe, I thought, just *maybe* the guy had some talent. Maybe the pictures would be worth looking at. And besides, I had told him that he needed my okay before he used my face.

"What happened to those pictures from last week?" I asked him, innocently enough. The rest of the team had gone off to the locker room, so I guess they didn't care.

Keith stopped fiddling with his camera and looked up at me. "Beats me," he said. "I've been too busy *reading*."

For a second we just stared at each other. I was at a loss for words. That shows you how surprised I was. I'm *never* at a loss for words.

Keith dropped out of the stare first. I think he felt embarrassed about his snappy reference to my put-down of the week before, though I guess I probably deserved it.

"Uh, they came out fine," he said, eyes dropping to his feet. "I've got them up in my locker if you want to see them."

"Any of me?" I couldn't help asking. I immediately felt as vain as every other girl on the team.

"Well, yes, the one."

"Okay, then, I want to check it out in case you use it."

I'm not sure even now why I bothered going up to Keith's locker to see only one picture. Certainly it wasn't because I had any interest in *him*. As far as I was concerned, Keith was still a jerk. But that didn't mean I wasn't curious about my picture.

In ten minutes I had changed into human clothes and made my way with Keith to the locker bank across from Mrs. Morris's room. Keith's locker was indistinguishable from the others on the outside, but inside it had a little more character. There was a reproduction of an Ansel Adams print, a Steichen photograph, and a fashion shot by Avedon. On the inside of the door were dozens of three-by-five cards, each with a saying typed on it. For instance:

Adults are obsolete children . . . and to hell with 'em.
—Dr. Seuss

I'd never join any club that would have me as a member.
—Woody Allen

The man who goes alone can start today, but he who travels with another must wait till that other is ready and it may be a long time before they get off.
—Thoreau

I was impressed. Even if Keith himself were permanently stuck in this piddling little burg, at least his mind had done some traveling.

While Keith got down the pictures, I continued a nonstop monologue that had begun with a few complaints about Mrs. Morris and ended with some comments on Woody Allen. I've noticed that these monologues can sometimes overwhelm people, but Keith seemed to handle it well.

When he opened the box of prints, my picture was sitting on top of the pile. It was great.

"That can't be me!" I said. "I look like I should be on the cover of some magazine."

"It's a good shot," Keith replied, pleased with his own work.

"But my arms look fat."

"They're not fat. It's a blur caused by the movement. That's what makes this an action shot, so people can see you're just about to hit the volleyball."

"Yeah," I said. "So are they going to use this in the yearbook?"

"I think so," Keith told me. "There's only one page for volleyball, so the editor says he'll use the group shot and one action shot. This is it."

I looked quickly through the other photographs in the box. They were good, but none of them had the pizzazz of me jumping for the ball. I could see why Keith had picked that one from all the rest.

"I still can't believe it. Could you make me a print of this? I'll pay you whatever . . ."

"You don't have to pay me a thing. I ran off a couple of prints before I got the cropping just right. Here." And he handed me an envelope with two prints inside.

"Well, thanks," I said, smiling at him for the first time. It seemed to me, then, that Keith giving me those prints was just about the nicest thing anyone had done for me in my six weeks at Wagnalls. It also seemed to me that Keith himself wasn't the total Piggie I had thought he was. There was a chance, an *anorexic* chance, that Keith might be worth knowing a little better.

So I stood there, silent, waiting for Keith to make a move. He stood across from me, his mouth half open as if he wanted to say something, but nothing came out of it except a little labored breathing. Maybe, I thought, the prospect of making some sort of move on me had paralyzed him. Emotional lockjaw. Maybe we'd be standing like this all afternoon if I didn't help him out.

"Well?" I said.

"Well, what?" he answered.

"Well, aren't you going to offer to walk me home?"

"Oh, sure," Keith said. He smiled as if he were terribly relieved.

Now I want to say, right off, that I did not like Keith much at this point. Basically, he looks ordinary—definitely no cause for heavy respiration—just your average guy. Besides that, Keith's level of articulation and witty repartee seemed somewhat below that of the typical gray-suited accountant. And this thumbnail evaluation doesn't even go into Keith's personality problems, which seemed overwhelming, though not very interesting.

And I didn't *need* Keith for male company. I was getting lots of attention from Pete Weyman and the other Cro-Magnon types at Wagnalls. But there was something about Keith's awkwardness that made him more attractive than those other guys who thought that foreplay meant hitting a girl on the head with a club. So I gave him a chance.

"You can protect me from the Riverdale Flasher," I said.

"Oh, sure," he said with a laugh.

"Really," I went on. "There's a guy in a raincoat who exposes himself over near the park. Nancy Suddaby saw him. She did an oral report on it in English."

"I can imagine. Pretty gross."

"The flasher?" I asked.

"No, Nancy Suddaby's report."

Keith smiled and I laughed. At least the two of us were in agreement about Nancy Suddaby. As we walked to my father's apartment, I found we were in agreement on a few hundred other things as well. Of course, I still did most of the talking, but Keith *was* able to say a few things, especially when I helped him along. Sometimes I can be nice, you know, so I prodded Keith periodically with questions to keep him going until we reached the apartment building.

"Must be a nice view," Keith said.

"Yeah. All the way to the dump on a clear day. We have the penthouse, you know." I don't know why I told him that, but I did.

"Must be nice."

"It's okay, but not great," I said, covering myself. "If there were a skyline like New York City, well, that would be worth it. But here the most interesting thing to see is the roof of the school."

"How do your parents like it?"

"My father likes it fine," I said. "And my mother's opinion doesn't count. She's dead," I told him. That was simplifying things a lot, but it was how I felt.

Keith got an expression on his face that was so apologetic it made me feel bad for lying. "Oh. Well, anyhow, you're here," he said. "No flashers on the way." Keith was looking awkward again, like he wanted me to invite him up but would run away if I actually suggested it.

"Disappointed?" I asked him.

"Sure. I could have protected you."

"How?"

"Oh, cover up your eyes, I guess."

I laughed and Keith smiled. The conversation had

stopped and now we were both feeling awkward. I guessed that any further moves were up to me.

"Thanks for walking me home," I said. Now I was the one searching for words. "And Keith, it was okay talking to you, you know."

He just looked at me, or, to be precise, at my knees.

"Maybe we can be friends," I said, holding out my hand.

It took him a second to realize that he was supposed to shake my hand and a few seconds more to actually do it. I liked the touch of his hand, soft and gentle like Keith himself. If Keith had been less of an Iggie, even he could have figured that out.

At the time, though, he was just confused.

"Sure. Friends," he said, almost as if he were talking to himself.

Chapter 7

KEITH

FRIENDS?

I spent a lot of time trying to figure out what friends could mean and finally decided that the word itself was ridiculous. Before Steven married Sandra, when they were just living together, my mother always introduced her as "Steven's, uh, friend," with some emphasis on the "uh" as if that explained everything. On the other hand, Uncle John sometimes walks into a classroom, his white shoes shining under the fluorescent lights, and declares that all of us are his friends. Even the checkout lady at the supermarket wears a little button that says she is my friend. Obviously "friends" is a much-abused word.

Back in October it wasn't entirely clear to me that I wanted Jane as a friend. I chalked up a quick list of fourteen things I didn't like about her, beginning with my aversion to freckles and ending with the fact that her voice sounds like a dump truck driving over gravel. Then it occurred to me that this kind of list-making wasn't doing me any good. Time to stop, I said to myself. Time to stop making lists and stop thinking about Jane.

I was busy thinking about not thinking about Jane when Frank popped into the yearbook cubbyhole to disturb my non-thoughts.

"Hey-hey. Whatchya doin'?"

"Looking at my shoes," I said.

"Yeah, I never noticed before but you got kinda big feet."

"Twelve and a halfs."

"I guess you gotta have big feet to fill your brother's shoes, huh?"

I thought about asking Frank to quietly disappear, but decided against it. "What's that supposed to mean?" I asked wearily.

"I don't know. Just makin' conversation. Hey, I hear that you're out hustling women. I mean, Jane Flemming's not bad for a beginner like you. You think you can handle all that?"

"Look, I just walked her home."

"Feet like those, maybe that's a good way to start. That's my way, too, you know. You start nice and easy, sort of feeling the whole thing out, if you know what I mean. Then you get the right signs, you know, and you make your move."

"Frank, there's really nothing going on between Jane and me. She wanted prints of the pictures I took of the volleyball team, that's all." I felt red in the face despite my cool words.

"Jeez, how much is she paying for the negatives? I mean, just what kind of pictures did you take?" Frank punctuated this with a dirty laugh.

"You're hopeless."

"No, I'm a nut-case. Big-mouth Marianne told me once I was . . . how'd she say it? Oh yeah, sexually upset."

"You mean sexually obsessed."

"Yeah, somethin' like that. She said I think about sex all the time, but she talks too big. One of these liberated types, eh? So I told her that sometimes I take a little time off and think about somethin' else, like maybe cars or football or somethin'. Maybe sex is only about 90 percent."

"You spend 90 percent of your time thinking about sex?"

"At least! I don't know about you intellectuals, you and Lou, maybe you spend a lot of time thinking about stamp collecting or French movies. But for the rest of us it's 90 percent sex."

I shook my head and tried to calculate my own percentage. I thought that 90 percent was a little high for me, though not because stamp collecting or the French cinema took up much mental space. I resolved to pay attention to my thoughts for the rest of the day and see how much time I actually did spend fantasizing about sex.

"Hey, Keith, let me give you a little advice about this Flemming broad," Frank said, plopping down in a swivel chair. "Girls like a guy who comes on strong, you know? After the preliminaries—how's that for a big word, huh?—well, don't waste your time trying to be a friend or anything. To hell with that respect-me stuff. You just give her some time to warm up and then come on."

"You're crazy," I said, turning red in the face at the mere idea.

"Hey, I do all right for myself. I bet you never . . ."

Frank leaned closer and whispered to me. This wasn't necessary in the otherwise empty room, but it added to the effect of his words.

"Did you? Did you?" he challenged me.

Not even close.

"Well, you can take it from somebody who knows, huh? The key to the whole thing is moving in quick. Be tough, 'cause that's what they like. Come on like Bogie."

"In *Casablanca?*"

"I don't know. The one where the guy stands in a trenchcoat and says 'Play it again, Sam.' "

"He never really said that, you know," I corrected.

"So who cares? All I'm saying is that you'll never get nowhere acting like Keith Hartman, the wimp. No offense. What they like is somebody who knows what he wants, huh? The next time you see Jane you gotta treat her as if you couldn't care less, and then, when she's dying for it, grab her."

I tried to picture myself in a trenchcoat, bending Jane backwards for a Hollywood kiss. The image seemed a little crazy but not unattractive. While I was daydreaming, the door from the hall opened and Lou Russell came loping into the room. He looked generally irritated.

"Looks like I found both of you," he began without sitting down. "Frank, where's that football article I was supposed to have? A deadline's a deadline, you know. I've got to have it by tomorrow so I can edit the masterpiece and mail it off."

"Right, I'll get it to you first thing," Frank said sheepishly.

"How about you head off to the gym right now and talk to Summerhays, huh? He says he hasn't even seen you yet. How are you going to write the story without talking to the coach?"

"Well, I was gonna . . ."

"Right now, Frank."

"Yes, sir," Frank said, saluting Lou and marching off.

Lou mumbled something I couldn't hear, then stretched out in the swivel chair.

"Keith, I wanted to see you about a couple of things, too. First off, we've got to fake some football pictures to fill up a page. The season scores are looking so bad that I'm going to blue-pencil them and save the team embarrassment. Can you get a couple of players in uniform and dummy up some shots?"

"Sure. I'll use Frank," I said.

"Well, how about a couple of real football players, okay? I'm leaving it up to you because you're going to be in charge anyway."

"Huh?" I said, wondering what he meant.

"I'm off to Boston and New York, doing the old college tour next week."

"So you're really applying to Harvard?"

"And why not, as Dan Aykroyd would say. My SAT's aren't stratospheric, but Uncle John says he'll write me a letter of application that'll knock the Ivies dead. Besides, I figure if your brother could get in, so can I."

"Yeah, but Steven didn't go."

"That was only one of the mistakes he made, Keith. If Harvard sends me the fat envelope, I'm not going to let romance stand in *my* way." The look Lou gave me suggested that he knew everything that had happened between Steven and Sandra. His next line suggested that he might even know more about Steven than I did.

"Your brother almost didn't graduate, you know."

"I heard it was a political thing after the cafeteria strike."

"Yeah, that's what he told everybody. But it really had to do with lousy attendance. Weasel was going to flunk him because he skipped too many classes. Now *that's* the real story."

"I didn't know that," I said.

"Steven didn't want people to know that," Lou went on. "He'd rather have people blinded by his personal brilliance—and I'm not even denying that he was brilliant. I mean, that guy ran the yearbook and the student council and half the other clubs at Wagnalls and still had time left over to pick up a bunch of A's and both the McCann twins. But there was another side . . ."

"How do you know all this?" I asked. I wondered just why Lou was shooting down my brother.

"Because my sister spent most of her high school career in love with him. Not that he'd pay attention to someone like her, just a plain student council treasurer. But she still used to cover for him. That flashy yearbook he did with all the color pages came out three grand in the red. The big cafeteria strike did nothing but change the concession company and throw two senile cafeteria supervisors out of work."

"But, Lou . . ."

"Look, Keith, I know you look up to your brother—and so do I. But it's been four years now and maybe it's time to see him a little more clearly than we used to. When I was a minor niner, Steven seemed like a superstar. I said to myself, 'Hey, I wanna be like that,' but of course nobody could live up to that image. Steven wasn't all stellar material, you know. There was a fair amount of common clay mixed in with that, the same stuff that you and I are made of. Same as Pescatore, too, though it hurts to admit it. What was your friend talking about when I came in?"

"He's not really my friend," I told him, my head still spinning from what he had said about Steven. "He was just giving me some advice."

"Pescatore?" Lou looked amazed. "On what?"

"Women."

"Oh my God. Next thing you know you'll be asking the school janitor for his comments on Baroque music. Take *my* advice . . ."

I think I would have, but the bell rang and sent both of us trudging to last period.

I definitely needed *somebody's* advice. I was wasting a lot of time and mental effort in not thinking about Jane. I knew perfectly well that there were lots of other things for me to worry about: the yearbook photos, the fact that I was out of developer, my miserable grade in history, a pimple acting out Vesuvius on my chin, not to mention energy, unemployment, and the fate of democracy in South America. It seemed to me that all of these deserved some portion of my attention. Unfortunately, all of my attention had a very different fixation. Jane.

There she was, standing by the old propeller-driven plane, sand blowing in her face as I took her in my arms. Here's looking at you, kid. She turns, grief-stricken, devastated as she walks to the plane. I tighten my trenchcoat, shoulders hunched against the wind . . .

I broke out of my fantasy and remembered Frank's 90 percent figure with a laugh. Maybe that was a conservative estimate.

If I had been more experienced with women I wouldn't have had to concentrate on Jane nearly so much, or so I thought. Experience would have given a polish to all my moves and buffed my technique to an effortless gleam. I tried to imagine Humphrey Bogart confused like me, wondering how to approach Ingrid Bergman and sweep her off her feet. But I just couldn't see it. The difference had to be experience.

My own experience was dismal. Carol Reilly was the last fiasco. I had tried the best I could to be entertaining. I actually memorized two jokes before the date, just in case. After the show, I talked about old movies, gossiped about the kids at school, tried to hold her hand, smiled until my gums hurt. I even told the two jokes.

It had been hopeless. Everything I said or did seemed to disappear into the void of her personality. She was like a black hole, absorbing all my energy and turning it into anti-matter. I realize all this now, though at the time I blamed myself, my deodorant, my breath, and at least twenty-two other items.

But somehow I had to blunder ahead with Jane. In a weird way, maybe Frank was right. Enough of this stupid "friends" stuff. Time to spice up our relationship with some flash, some passion. Jane was attractive, available, sexy. I was, uh, well at least I was available. I decided to approach Jane at her locker. That meant risking sweaty palms and shaky knees, but it beat calling her up on the phone.

After the last class, it was time to make my move. I walked over to Jane's locker while the usual end-of-day mob scene played itself out in the halls. Jane was always late, so that gave me a few minutes to perfect my approach. I would be direct, tough, I-couldn't-care-less, now or never, sexy. What did I have to lose?

She came up to her locker.

"Jane," I said. *Hello* wasn't tough enough.

"Hi, Keith."

"You and me," I said. "How about you and me go out Friday night?" Tough, aloof, cool. My hands were sweating like crazy.

"Huh?"

Oh, no, I thought, I've got to do it again. "I said, do you want to go out Friday night?" I didn't think my voice was nearly as tough, aloof, and cool the second time.

"You mean on a date?"

"I mean, uh . . ." Well, what did I mean? I started looking down at my feet, a bad sign. "Are you busy Friday or something?"

"Keith, are you trying to come on to me?" Jane was looking at me with a smile I could only describe as maternal.

"Well, uh, I don't know." So much for the Bogart approach.

"Hey, it's not one of those in-between things. Either this invitation is going to be a date, you know, with a capital 'D' and everything that goes with that, or else,

I don't know, or else you just want some company. Now which one is it?"

"Capital 'D.' "

"Look, Keith, I'm sorry. I just can't handle that. I mean, I'm sorry if it looked like I was leading you on or something, but that wasn't what I had in mind. I'm interested in you, and I like you, but, I like you as a person. Can you follow that?"

I wanted to shrink into my shoes. I saw a movie like that once, the *Incredible Shrinking Man*. One minute the guy's face-to-face with a friend, the next minute he's crawling out of his shoes, two inches tall.

"You said you wanted to be my friend."

"I still do, but that's different from being your lover or your girlfriend or anything like that."

"I didn't . . ."

"I know you didn't, but you know what I mean. I think we've got a lot in common and really get along well with each other. But I'd prefer to keep the whole thing nonromantic. Besides . . ." She bit her lower lip.

"Besides what?"

"Besides a lot of things. Look, I really didn't want to talk about this, you know, but I'm already seeing another guy and we have sort of a relationship."

"Oh."

"He's twenty-four. A grad student."

"Uh-huh," I said. If I were only two inches tall, I could scurry under one of the lockers and hide until it was all over.

"Really, I feel bad about this," Jane said in a more matter-of-fact voice. "I still want to be your friend, Keith, please try to understand that. I just want to keep us out of the whole boy-girl-your-place-or-mine thing. It's this syndrome of sex that poisons the whole thing. You know what I mean?" She took my lifeless hand in her own and squeezed it.

"Sure." I looked up at her for just a second, saw that she was looking back at me, then dropped my eyes back down to my shoes. They are very big shoes.

"Walk me home," she said, almost cheerfully. I think she was trying to pretend that everything was back to normal between us after this little episode of insanity on my part.

"I can't," I lied. "I've got to talk to Lou about a yearbook thing and it'll take a while."

"I'll wait."

"No, no," I went on, panic-stricken. "It could be an hour or more to lay this thing out."

I turned and walked awkwardly down the hall. I don't think I had ever been more aware of my feet, of the noise they made against the waxed floors, of how much they weighed as I tried to take each step.

Chapter 8

JANE

All right, I lied. I'm not even sure why I lied to Keith about having a boyfriend, except maybe that there was too much anxiety in the whole situation. I had an analyst once who said that my lying was a defense mechanism, a coping mechanism. I told him that I didn't have to lie to anybody just to cope. But, of course, that was a lie too.

I was stunned when Keith started coming on to me. It has to be an evolutionary flaw that your typical adolescent male is unable to handle a concept as simple as friendship. When I told Keith that I wanted to be his friend, I didn't mean *girl*friend, I meant friend. Why can't people accept what you say as just what you say? Why does everybody have to read *into* things?

What did I feel about Keith? Well, I'll have to admit that he gave me a little buzz right from the first day he walked me home. But in October Keith was a long way from developing into a major buzz, much less a real vibration. The most accurate thing I could say about Keith at the time was that he had potential. On the positive side, Keith had brains and talent. There was some real evidence of life in his cortex, which is a lot more than can be said for most of the guys in a school where a lobotomy would be redundant.

On the negative side, Keith was still sort of a nerd. He was too ordinary to make much of an impression. It goes back to his face. If Keith held up a gas station, nobody could describe him because he has no distinguishing features. The only vaguely interesting item about Keith's appearance is his eyes, but most of the time he uses them to stare at his feet. He has big, big feet.

Socially, Keith was a nobody. To say that Keith had kept a low profile at Wagnalls would be an exaggeration. He had *no* profile. It was almost as if, unable to follow Steven Hartman's one-man show, Keith had gotten off the stage altogether and gone off to live by himself in the woods. Not that there's anything wrong with living in the woods, something Thoreau made respectable two hundred years ago, but it doesn't add much to one's social charisma.

Is it possible for someone like me to have a boyfriend with negligible charisma? You gotta be kidding! Keith is a nice guy, but I wasn't going to have anyone as prosaic as that for my first boyfriend at Wagnalls.

So I lied to him. It's my favorite escape hatch. I realize that lying is nothing to be proud of, but it works. Lying has given me the ability to change my relatively pathetic existence into the substance of a hundred Harlequin romances. Even as a kid, I was a virtuoso at lying. I remember taking the 5th Avenue bus with Marci and making up these wild stories about being molested by my uncle. The little old ladies carrying their packages up from Bloomingdale's couldn't help but listen in. We finally had to stop that game when a social work student horned in and began insisting that I get off at St. Luke's for a medical examination.

When I started going to Strath in Toronto I developed an entire fantasy society. While the other little debs were running off to their Serbo-Croatian Balles, I was busy with an international jet set that made them green with envy. I even arranged to have letters mailed to me from places like Geneva and Marrakesh to make it all more convincing.

I'm not sure that these lies ever got me very far at Strath, or anywhere else for that matter, but they worked to draw attention away from my problems in real life. My mother had left us—disappeared, for all intents and purposes—and my father was on the skids at work. How could I talk about that? The truth would leave me wide open. Instead I complained about getting ditched by the son of a diplomat from Kuwait or not being invited to the film festival at Monte Carlo. I could handle these problems since they were entirely my inventions.

It was easy to make up a graduate student boyfriend to keep Keith at a distance. Keith was so quickly taken in by my imaginary boyfriend that he didn't even ask any questions about him. He didn't give me a chance to work out the details of my fantasy. Of course, creating a fantasy life has never been a problem; only real life is a problem.

In real life, a guy named Pete Weyman was trying to

make an entrance into this improvisatory drama I call daily living. Most guys in real life make rotten entrances. Like Keith, they get all confused about what they're trying to do and end up blowing their lines. Pete Weyman wasn't like that. He was never confused about what he was trying to do. His intentions were clear from the start. And they were entirely dishonorable.

I would have sent Pete off yelping, tail between his legs, if he weren't so absolutely gorgeous. I confess that his looks really did make a difference. Not that I went out with him right away, mind you, but I didn't discourage him totally.

Pete Weyman happened to have a certain amount of status at Wagnalls H.S. and you never know when a high-status boyfriend might come in handy. If I actually had to make an appearance at something like a prom, then a real person like Pete might be far more useful than an imaginary grad student. So I didn't dismiss Pete, I put him on ice. I told him that my father had grounded me for two weeks. I figured that would be enough time for me to figure out what I wanted to do with him.

Actually, my father hasn't grounded me in years. I think he got scared once when I O.D.'d on some Valium, about six months after my mother took off. Pretty stupid, eh? As if a suicide attempt would bring her back. But Golden Voice took the threat seriously, got me into analysis faster than the ambulance got me to St. Luke's, and ever since he's been a little afraid of me. Maybe that little episode is one of the reasons we don't get along.

"Are you getting on any better at school, Jane?" my

father boomed at me. It was a couple days after Weyman asked me out, maybe a week after Keith had made his big move.

"Same."

"Met anyone interesting yet?"

My father has had a disproportionate interest in my friends ever since Marci got pregnant in Grade 9.

"Dream on. One guy did ask me out, though."

"What's he like?" my father asked. I guess it was his way of showing interest.

"He's an animal," I said, exaggerating as usual.

"Oh?"

"That's what the kids say. Of course, any guy around here who knows how to French would probably be called an animal."

"Do you have to be crude, Jane?"

"You asked," I said. It was true, he did. I didn't start it. I never start it—I just fan the fire.

"I thought you weren't going to go out with that kind of boy any more."

"It's my life," I said, wondering why he should care. I think my father has seen every aspiring male in my life as some kind of potential sex maniac.

"Then why ruin it?"

"Who says I'm going to ruin anything?"

"Look, I just don't want any more phone calls from the emergency room."

"Why won't you let me forget that?" I asked.

"Sorry, I . . . uh," he answered. Golden Voice felt guilty now.

"Why don't you come right out and say what's eating you. It's my virginity that you're worried about."

"I just worry when you go out with a boy you yourself describe as an animal."

"I never said that I was going to go out with him."

"Then what are we talking about?" he asked.

"My virginity."

"Jane!"

Obviously my father and I did not have normal conversations, we had running arguments. In a conversation, it doesn't matter who starts it or how it goes ahead, or who finishes it. But in an argument, all these things count. They determine the winner—and the winner always had to be me. Always.

"I called your mother from the station today," he began again. I think he'd been searching all along for some way to break this to me.

"My mother is dead," I muttered.

"Jane, cut it out. You're the one who won't talk with her now."

"Yeah, but *she* was the one who walked out. You can tell her that, too. She started this whole mess—don't let her forget that," I said. I'd never forget. The cruddy little note. A year of wondering after that—no letters, no phone calls, nothing. Then suddenly she's well again and wants to talk. She thinks I should turn my back on all that hurt, on that whole awful year, but I never will. I'll never get even for that.

"She knows that, Jane," my father said. "You rub it in every time you won't talk to her. You think that doesn't hurt her?"

I turned away. The hurt was on both sides. I could have said that, I could have admitted that, but it would have left me wide open and I won't do that any more. Never again.

"I'm surprised she talks to you," I said, taking control again. "Talk about hurting people."

"Jane, I—"

"Right. Try and defend yourself. You sent her right over the edge, maybe even pushed her up to it. Caught right at it in the studio, weren't you? I *saw* the note she left."

"That's enough, Jane!" Boom. Thunder.

"That's what did it to her last time," I said, not letting up on him. "You and the receptionist going at it right in the studio."

"That's enough, Jane."

"It's all right to do it but not to talk about it, huh? Nice double standard."

"Stop being a bitch."

"Golden Voice is reduced to swearing?"

"You know what I mean."

"Yeah, I know what you mean. What you mean is that you want to be let off the hook, after you drove her crazy, after you drove her away. You want me to forgive and forget. Kiss-kiss and everything's just peachy. But everything isn't just peachy because of what *you* did."

He was getting really mad now. I could see him getting all red in the face and the muscles tightening in his neck.

"It wasn't just me," he said through gritted teeth.

"Oh, yeah. Toss it off. Maybe it was me, maybe it was the man-in-the-moon. You'll never admit what you did. You drove my mother crazy, you . . . you . . . God, I wish you were dead."

And then I ran out of the room. I raced down the hallway to my bedroom and threw myself on the bed, smashing my hand against the bedstead as I fell forward. The physical pain was good for me. It was a focus for that other pain, the pain inside. I gripped my injured hand in the other and willed all the pain into it, all the problems, all the grief, all the past.

It helped.

Chapter 9

KEITH

I ENDED UP GOING TO THE WOODY ALLEN DOUBLE bill by myself. I thought the movies might do something to counteract the depression that was taking root in my soul. But I was wrong.

Going to the movies was a mistake. I kept looking at the other people in line, the couples joking and playing around with each other, the packs of kids without dates scanning the crowd for someone to pick up. The whole scene made me miserable.

Up on the screen, inside the dark theater, Woody Allen was getting stuffed with bananas from a berserk machine. The sequence convulsed almost everybody in the theater. I couldn't even smile. I wanted *Bananas* to finish so that my own favorite film could begin; I wanted *Play It Again, Sam.* It isn't one of Woody Allen's best films—not as witty as *Love and Death* and not nearly as brilliant as *Manhattan*—but it's the one I like best. It was the one I wanted to see with Jane.

As Woody Allen was rejected on screen by woman

after woman, I could see the rest of my life unfolding. There I was, magnified fifty times life size, waxing pathetic to the giggles of the audience. And there was Diane Keaton comforting the defeated Woody Allen. And there she was again, coming back to the apartment to see him, to surrender herself to whatever it was in Woody Allen that she found attractive. The screen grew dark, then Allen and Keaton reappeared, in bed now, and Woody delivered one of the great lines: "That was the most fun I ever had without laughing."

I wasn't laughing. My eyes were wet and I felt even more depressed than before. I didn't want to wait until Woody Allen would give Keaton back to his lifelong friend. I just didn't want to see it.

So for the first time in my life I walked out on a Woody Allen film. The theater lobby was empty when I left. The parking lot still and cold. I felt absolutely alone.

What I needed was work. I woke up Saturday morning and knew I had to do something to take my mind off Jane. The darkroom was the answer. I mixed the chemicals with exaggerated care, dusted the enlarger and cleaned the lens, even read the instructions packed with the paper—all to keep from thinking. I began by printing some shots from the previous week, a mixture of my own work and pictures taken for the yearbook. I enjoyed the rhythms of the darkroom and the smell of the chemicals.

I had forgotten that Lou Russell was coming over with some negatives and remembered only when the doorbell rang upstairs. My father brought him down to where I was working.

"Hi, Lou," I said, poking my head out of the darkroom curtains.

"My God, look at that pipe organ!" Lou replied, not even turning in my direction.

"It's my father's toy," I explained.

"Fantastic. I've never seen an honest-to-God pipe organ in somebody's house before and, I mean, it's down here in the basement rec room. Of all the places to put it." Lou was already sitting down at the console and depressing keys on the first manual.

"Do you play?" I asked.

"Not organ. Piano. I hate those little electric organs with the autorhythm units and the tacky arrangements of 'Smoke Gets in Your Eyes.' But this . . . this is something else. So your father is playing Bach?"

"And Buxtehude."

"I'm envious, Keith, really envious. Do you play?"

"No, I took violin for a while and dropped it. I don't think I'm very musical. Then again, neither is my father. What he really enjoyed was installing the thing and now he plays it simply because it's here. I think he likes the mechanism more than the music." I had liked that particular line ever since Steven made it up.

"Where'd it come from?" asked Lou, still staring at the console.

"A church about fifty miles from here. They bought an electronic one and sold this to my father for almost nothing. It took him a good two years to install it."

"I can believe it," he said, staring at the array of pipes.

"Now where are those negatives I'm supposed to print up?"

"Oh, yeah," Lou said, his mind snapping back from

somewhere else. He unzipped his vinyl briefcase and pulled out some glassine envelopes with crayoned X's to mark the negatives he wanted me to print.

I looked carefully at the negatives. "These are all a little thin," I said with just a touch of superiority.

"What does that mean?"

"It means that Charlie either underexposed the shot or didn't develop them long enough. The print will end up low in contrast, but I'll do what I can to compensate."

"You're the expert. I've only got one request."

I looked up.

"Can I watch?"

Lou stayed until lunchtime, supervising the dozen prints he needed and even processing a few himself. He seemed to be as interested in the magical operations of the darkroom as I was, or at least interested enough to stand for a long time stooped over in a posture that would have put most people into traction.

"I guess that's everything," Lou said. We were watching the last prints washing in a laundry tub.

"Yeah. They should be ready by tonight if you're in a hurry, or I'll bring them in on Monday," I offered.

"I'll wait for them," he said. "I guess you were printing some of your own stuff before I came over." He had fished two wet prints out of the washtub.

"Yeah, I've been doing my own work for three years now."

"Are they all this good?" he asked, studying the prints. "I like the effect, here, where the light comes up from behind."

Lou seemed so impressed with the prints that I

debated whether or not to show him the portfolio I'd been working on for the past two years. So far I had only shown it to my brother Steven, who was not at all impressed, but then Steven knew nothing about photography. I didn't think Lou knew much about photography either, but he did seem interested.

"If you've got a minute," I said, hesitating only a little, "I'll show you this portfolio I've been putting together."

"I've got an hour," he said, checking his watch.

I pulled out the big package of mounted prints, handed them to Lou, and stood back in silence while he made his way through them.

The silence was awful. I waited quietly at first, then tried to busy myself cleaning up the darkroom. I thought the portfolio was pretty good but I was still nervous and my hands were sweating badly.

"Well, what do you think?" I ventured.

"They're great," he said quietly.

"What?"

"I said," Lou repeated as I began smiling, "that they're great. If I had any idea that you were doing this quality of work, I would have personally dragged you onto the yearbook staff years ago. And you hide your talent. How many people have seen this portfolio?"

"Steven and, uh, you, and that's it, I guess."

"You see what I mean? Now some of these prints are just incredible, like this." Lou brought out a shot of the moon rising over a misty lake, perhaps my single best photograph.

"I did that with my Olympus," I explained, "though it looks like I used a large-format camera. The moon was the toughest part. You know, it only takes up three tenths of an arc degree but looks much larger . . ."

"You're getting too technical for me," Lou broke in. "All I know is that this shot is great, and some of these others, too. You shouldn't just be showing them to me. You should get them into a contest or arrange a show at a gallery."

"I guess," I said, loving every word.

"And one thing you have to do for me," Lou said, "you have to shoot the opening section of the yearbook. We need a big photo spread for the front, the full sixteen pages. I'll get little Charlie Fisher to do the candid shots. I want you working on the important photography."

"Well, thanks, Lou . . ."

"Don't thank me yet. There's a catch. Mrs. Morris has picked the theme for the book, so that has to be the theme for your opening spread."

"What is it?"

"Personal Growth," Lou said with a wry smile.

"You're kidding."

"Wish I was. Morris is dead-set on it, so there's not much I can do. She's busy selecting bits of Wordsworth to sprinkle in with the photographs, but don't let that bother you. They might just get lost at the printers. What we need is an idea for a series of photographs that'll connect with this growth B.S. and yet take us right through the school. Now *there's* a challenge for you." Lou was smiling at me.

Maybe a challenge was just what I needed, or maybe the praise went right to my head, but I felt better after talking to Lou. Jane no longer took up 100 percent of my mental space, not even 90 percent, because I was concentrating on the idea of a photo series. There were hundreds of ways to handle the job, but the stupid theme kept getting in the way of my ideas. What on earth was "Personal Growth"?

Chapter 10

JANE

I WANT TO SAY THAT MY GOING OUT WITH PETE Weyman had *nothing* whatsoever to do with Keith. In my mind, they were in two separate categories—Keith was Keith and Weyman was, well, a hunk. See? No connection.

I didn't even go out with Pete Weyman because I liked him very much. Basically, Pete is a mouth-breather, a type I usually never look at twice. His attempts at conversation suggested an IQ the size of my bank balance—and that is pretty *low*. And he was a football player. What a cliché! So when Pete first started making moves, I had a hard time taking him seriously. The last thing I had in my mind was actually going out with him.

So how come I changed my mind?

Good question, Jane. Good question.

The psychological explanation is that I went out with Weyman to spite my father. This is consistent with a good four years of getting even with Golden

Voice, a behavior of mine that has been pointed out by psychiatrists, teachers, social workers, and even Marci Jackson. The fact that I called Pete up the day after I fought with my father also supports this explanation. I mean, Pete Weyman is pretty sexy in real life, but he became almost infinitely desirable as soon as my father found him dangerous.

Yet I had all this figured out when I called Pete, so obviously there was more to it than simple revenge against Golden Voice. I think Nancy Suddaby had something to do with it too.

How embarrassing!

I had merely mentioned in the locker room that Weyman had tried to ask me out when Nancy Suddaby and the rest of the team went into an orgy of pure envy. "Must be nice! I bet! Oh, wow! God knows why he asked you out!" I couldn't quite figure out how Weyman could have a reputation as an animal and still be regarded as the most desirable guy in Grade 12. Can an animal really be a hunk?

So I went out with him. To the movies. At least it wasn't the same night Keith went to the movies. If he had seen me with Weyman, Keith would have overdosed on Kodak developer and been found comatose on his darkroom floor. But I didn't know that, then. I didn't know how important I was to him. Back then, Keith was a friend and Weyman was a hunk. And that was that.

Golden Voice answered the door when Pete showed up for the date. "Good evening. You must be Pete Weyman," he said. My father is brilliant at disguising his disgust, but I knew he was checking Pete for hairy palms when they shook hands.

"Yes, sir. I just wanted to tell you how much I enjoy your radio show."

What a line of bull! My father's call-in show comes on at ten in the morning and nobody under the age of forty-five *ever* listens to it.

"Thank you. It seems very popular from the ratings," my father said. The old charmer was charmed himself.

I checked myself out in the mirror while they talked. I felt sexy as hell. My jeans were so tight that I had to lie down on the bed and zip them up with a coat hanger. If I gained one more pound I'd have to give them up altogether. My sweater didn't need the same effort to get into, but it had the same effect. Like spray paint. I figured it would be just the thing for a somebody like Weyman. The careful way he avoided looking at me as long as my father was around showed that I had him pegged just right.

Now the question might come up, why tease him like that? I had no intention of taking Pete Weyman seriously. He was too young, too plebeian, too stupid, and maybe too much an animal. But I wanted to see how he'd react. My problem, really, is curiosity. You know what it does to cats. I wanted to see if I could really get this small-town Casanova all hot and bothered. In fact, I wondered what a small-town Casanova might be like.

Pete uttered his first romantic line to me as we were waiting for the elevator. "Hey, you really look, uh, just great."

I watched Pete as he eyeballed me up and down, and then checked myself out in the flecked mirrors by the elevator. It occurred to me that I looked pretty sleazy. I took out a cigarette to complete the image, then turned to examine my date.

Let me take a minute out here and say a few words about Pete Weyman: Wagnalls's version of ideal manhood. First off he resembles Christopher Reeve so much that if he had on a Superman outfit I imagine he could take me on an aerial tour of the whole town.

The adjective that really fits Weyman best is "big." Big shoulders, big jaw, big muscles in the arms. In fact, his jeans were tight enough to advertise the fact that he was big all over. At least that's one way to put it.

This is not to say that Weyman's appearance was without flaws. His eyes were really too small for his face—almost beady—and his forehead suggested a Cro-Magnon look. Also he was blond, and blonds are boring.

Pete drove his *father's* red Camaro. It was enough to make you wonder about the old man.

"How d'you like my shirt?" he asked.

"It's interesting." The design looked like a bunch of chrysanthemums littered over a purple ground.

"See these things?" he said, pointing with one finger at some gold jewelry dangling around his neck while he steered the car with his other hand.

"Yeah."

"They're a phallic symbol. From Polynesia. That's what the guy said."

"Oh," I responded. I might have said something like *pretty subtle* or *gross me out the door,* but I resisted the temptation. For just a second I thought about Keith who, despite his other problems, can at least find one or two civilized things to talk about.

Pete drove me to the twin theater at the mall just outside of town. I was hoping he might take me to the new Jack Nicholson film at the West Cinema, but instead he paid for tickets to the latest Clint Eastwood movie on the other side. Groan. I would have said something right then if I hadn't been so busy observing the crowd. Margie Saltzman was there with two friends. They watched Pete with undisguised and never-to-be-fulfilled lust and waved to me without any real envy because their case was hopeless. Nancy Suddaby was over buying popcorn but she pretended not to see me.

Good.

There isn't too much to be said about the movie. I think 120 people died in the first twenty minutes—and then it got *really* violent. I spent most of the movie looking at my watch and wondering when Pete's hand would make a move off my shoulder. After a half hour, I figured the arm was to all intents and purposes frozen. I leaned my head against Pete's shoulder and nestled a little closer to see if this might get the arm going. In the process I was almost knocked out by English Leather fumes.

Pete seemed to find new inspiration after I moved in on him. His right hand reached down and grabbed my breast, holding it like a football. I waited for some additional move, but there wasn't any. He held on like a linebacker running towards a touchdown.

"Why don't you buy some popcorn?" I suggested.

"Huh?"

"Popcorn. Buy some," I said, moving so he lost his grip on me.

Pete went off as instructed and I was left alone for a

few minutes. On screen, Clint Eastwood was punching out some poor sucker in a blue suit. He did this with the same kind of nonchalance some people have blowing bubble gum. It was disgusting—not so much the punching; the nonchalance.

"Here," Pete said as if he was irritated at having missed the movie.

No butter. As if I was going to eat this lousy, day-old popcorn without butter. As if I wasn't worth the extra fifty cents to make the popcorn edible.

"There's no butter," I whispered.

"So?"

"I like butter." I handed the box back to him. I was tempted to pour it on his head but I had a hunch, just a hunch, that he'd slug me.

"Look, the movie's at the good part," he said. Clint Eastwood was riddling somebody with a machine gun.

"Get some," I said in a voice well over a whisper. I was angry and so was he. But I won. Pete slunk off to get what I wanted and I slumped back down in my seat, propping my legs over the seats in front. Why are guys such drips?

The movie ended about the same time the popcorn ran out. Pete said he wanted to go someplace for a drink, but I didn't feel like going through the no-I.D. hassle. Then he offered me some weed, as if marijuana were some really exotic plant around here.

Pete turned on the car so we could get some heat and lit up a j. I sucked up the smoke and felt pretty much nothing at all. Pete was acting like he was getting stoned right out of his head, which only says a lot for the power of suggestion.

We were midway through the j when he reached for

me. Ever awkward! I mean, making out in a car with bucket seats and a gearshift between them has got to be a feat for contortionists.

"Hey, I like you, you know," he said in a kind of throaty whisper. Maybe his voice was supposed to be full of passion.

"Yeah?"

"Yeah, really. You've got class and . . ."

I figured he was searching for some romantic phrase that would just make me melt in his arms.

". . . and you're not like the other girls around here."

Oh, well. He tried.

"C'mere."

Pete's first kiss was quite nice; dry, soft, even a touch romantic. It was the second one that was the killer. I thought his tongue was going to give me a tonsillectomy.

"Pete," I said when I could talk again.

"Yeah."

"We better go. My father's been leaning on me lately."

"In a little while," he said.

Jeez. In a little while I would be dead from carbon monoxide fumes, suffocated by English Leather, and permanently damaged by Pete's tongue.

"Now, Pete," I said, firmly enough it seemed to me.

"Just a second," he said, crushing his lips against mine. This time his teeth hurt me and his hands were grabbing at everything within reach. I was about to open the door and get out when Pete backed off.

"Did you like that?" he asked, putting the car into gear.

"I thought the movie was the pits," I told him.

"Not the movie."

"Oh, well . . ." I didn't know what to say. He really was kind of an animal.

"I thought you would," he concluded proudly.

Yecch!

Chapter 11

KEITH

I DIDN'T LEARN THAT JANE HAD GONE OUT WITH Pete Weyman for over a month after the event itself. There was no particular reason that anyone who knew should mention it to me. In retrospect, I guess it's just as well that I didn't find out about it. Misery is one thing, abject misery is something else.

I tried, as best I could, to put Jane out of my mind. It occurred to me that she had absolutely no right to be there—in my mind—and ought to be exiled to someplace else—like out in the middle of the Gobi Desert. I kept busy with other things in the hope that mental congestion would crowd out any thoughts of Jane. And it worked. A little.

I thought a lot about the stupid yearbook theme, "Personal Growth." It's one of those phrases you can't really get hold of, like the Blob in that old Steve McQueen movie or the slime in *X from Outer Space*. Personal growth? It sounds like the sort of thing you ought to have surgically removed. How could I possibly handle it with a bunch of black and white photographs?

The answer finally came to me when I was leafing through a book of photographs by Duane Michals. Then the whole approach came to me in a real rush. I went racing off to the yearbook office with the idea pretty clear in my own mind, but I brought the Michals book along to help explain it to Lou.

Unfortunately, Frank got his hands on the book first. "Will ya take a look at the bod on this one! And you're trying to tell me this is art?" he exclaimed.

I hadn't actually told Frank anything, but I thought the book should be treated with a little more respect than what he might offer a *Penthouse* centerfold.

"I tell you," Frank went on, "this may be art, but this girl here . . ." Frank turned the book around so that Lou could see the page he was describing, "she's got really nice, uh, memories."

"Mammaries, Frank," I corrected.

"You know, Frank," Lou said, "there's something really incongruous about anything polysyllabic coming out of your mouth, even if your father is running for mayor."

"Did he insult me?" Frank asked me. "Did he?"

"Keith," Lou said, ignoring him, "I can't see how Duane Michals is going to help us deal with Personal Growth."

"This girl's giving me a growth," Frank threw in.

"Come on, Frank, get serious," I said, ready to lay out my plan to both of them. "Here's the idea—a series of photographs that follows a phantom girl around the school, from the first floor right up to the science lab. I'll superimpose the location shots so the girl becomes a kind of dream, sort of phantasmagorical."

"Fanta what?" Frank asked.

"I think I can see it," Lou said. "You'd be juxtaposing the dream and reality, and the camera would be searching. The camera would be you, all of us, reaching out for the dream."

"Well, yeah," I said, not sure that I had even figured all that out yet.

"I just wanna know what your model's gonna wear, huh? You gonna have her go around naked, then I wanna help."

"Frank, I've got to hand it to you," Lou laughed. "You have the most lascivious mind I've ever run across."

"Thank you, thank you. What did he say?"

"He said you're very clever," I lied. "But the girl is going to wear clothes, maybe a ballet outfit."

"Awwh," Frank said. "You intellectuals should stick to stamp collecting."

"How about you get out of here before you're late to next class," Lou said as the bell went off. "Keith, hold up for a minute."

I waited until Frank had gone off to hear what Lou had to say. I figured it was probably important—and in many ways it was.

"Have you got a model yet?" he asked.

"Uh, no," I said. Not that I didn't have ideas, but I was nowhere near a willing body.

"Why not ask that New York girl you like? It might be a way to make a start."

"I think that's already finished."

"Don't give up so easily. Relationships don't start

and finish, they go in circles. Why not ask her to model for you? She can only say no."

"And then?"

"Then you keep on asking until she says yes. Go find her."

So I found her. Jane was stacking books in her locker at the end of the day to protect them from Wagnalls's book-eating mice. I said something like "Hi" and Jane went into a long monologue on Mrs. Morris's latest intellectual atrocity. I think she went on talking for a good five minutes before I could say another word.

"By the way," she finally asked me, "did you want something?"

I tried to handle that with my usual nonchalance—sweaty hands, pounding heart, tied tongue. I was pathetic and I wasn't even asking her out.

"I was, uh, wondering if you could help me on a project."

"I guess. Make me an offer."

"Huh?" I said. If Jane thought I was clueless before this, every word I said seemed to reinforce the impression.

"Offer to buy me a drink or lunch. In New York, these things are always put together over lunch."

"But it's too late for lunch. And I'm too young to drink," I said, feeling all panicky.

"Well, then, improvise."

"Uh, how about . . ." and I wracked my brain . . . "how about we go to the Parkside?" Inspiration at last.

"What's that? A bar?"

"No."

"Well, what?"

"You've got to see it to believe it," I said, finally feeling in charge of things.

"Nothing gross, huh?"

"No, nothing like that. Come on."

My inspiration was about ten minutes away from the school—an ice cream parlor right out of a thirties movie. It wasn't a careful re-creation by some coast-to-coast chain; the Parkside was a genuine throwback to the days when ice cream parlors were the center of high school social life.

"I don't believe it," Jane whispered in awe.

"Bet you don't have any of these left in New York," I said. The booths were oak, scratched with the initials of generations—my parents' included. The ceiling was painted tin, the floor a checkered pattern of asphalt tile. Over at the counter, past the lineup of red stools and standing just behind the goosenecked soda water taps, was an ancient man who hadn't moved since we walked in.

"Is the old guy stuffed?" Jane whispered.

"No, he's real. That old guy has been running the place since 1930. Shhh—here he comes."

The old man walked over at a pace so incredibly slow that I could have told Jane my entire photo idea before he reached our booth. I decided not to. The suspense was working in my favor.

"I'll have the Parkside sundae," I told the old guy. "It's heavy on the chocolate," I explained to Jane.

"Zit city," she replied. "I'll have a Heavenly Delight and a coffee for each of us."

The ancient soda jerk walked carefully back behind the counter to work his ice cream magic. Jane had finished two cigarettes and a long story about Weasel's incompetence by the time he brought our sundaes.

"Wow—it's real whipped cream," Jane said, digging in.

"How many places still put it on with a scoop?" I asked her.

"How many places have Methuselah as a soda jerk? Now, Keith, how about you lay out this project and I'll figure out whether I'll help you."

"Take a look at this," I said, handing her the book of Duane Michals's photographs. She took some time with it while I busied myself scraping chocolate sauce from the bottom of the sundae dish.

"This," I explained, "is what gave me the idea for Personal Growth."

"What?"

"For the yearbook. Remember I told you about the opening photo section and the theme Mrs. Morris picked out? Well, Lou's going to use a Ferlinghetti poem as an intro and I want to do a series of maybe twenty photographs like those in the book. Sort of dreamlike. We'd do all the shooting in the school, using the classrooms and gyms and places like that as backdrops."

"Backdrops to what?"

"Well, this is the part that's hard to explain. You see, each picture would have this girl as, uh, a kind of phantom. And she'd be half in the picture and half dissolved, like this picture in the book." I pointed to one of Michals's photos, a double exposure which gave the impression that the nude was more ghost than human.

"I think I get it," Jane said, biting her lip. "And

what is this model supposed to represent? Maturity? Growth? Sex? What?"

"Yeah, all those things," I said, grinning at her.

"You're gonzo," she said. "Who's going to be the model?"

I looked at her directly and said nothing.

"Me?" she shrieked. "No way! If you think I'm going to take my clothes off and dance starkers around the school cafeteria, you better take your brains in for dialysis."

"No, no," I said. "You wouldn't have to do it nude. You'd wear some sort of costume. Something ethereal, you know."

"Like a negligee with nothing underneath?"

"Jane, you've got a one-track mind. I thought guys were the ones who thought about sex all the time."

"Just shows how much you know. Look, Keith, I don't mean to dump on the whole idea, but I'm really not the right girl to model for you. I mean, look at me . . . do I look ethereal?"

It wasn't a question that I had really thought about before. While silence fell between us, I tried to consider Jane as a model. I studied her face, the innocence of freckles versus the corruption of too much makeup. Then I looked down at the rest of her, at Jane's square shoulders and large breasts. It seemed to me that her body suggests lots of things, but nothing very ethereal.

"See what I mean?" Jane said, annoyed by my stare. "My hips are too big for what you want. You don't need a lady wrestler for this pictorial, you want a ballet dancer."

"You don't look like a lady wrestler to me," I said.

It seemed to me that I was blushing for no sensible reason.

"Well, thanks," she said, sipping her coffee. "I know the kind of girl you want, though. You need somebody like Jill Hawes, you know, the cheerleader with the long blond hair? She'd be perfect."

"But . . ." I began, terrified at the prospect of having to approach the most desirable girl in the school. It had been hard enough to ask Jane.

"Relax. I'm certain she's vain enough to do it. So long as I'm there to supervise."

"Huh?"

"Sure. She'd never agree to it unless there was somebody like me there to look after her. Besides, you're going to need help setting up the shots and the lights."

"I guess."

"So give me the book so I can explain the idea to her," Jane ordered. "Better yet," she said, looking down at one of the nude photos, "you keep the book. I'll just talk to her about the idea."

"So you think it could work?"

"Keith, I think you could make almost anything work," Jane said. The compliment was just beginning to make my head swell when she finished up. "With my help."

Chapter 12

JANE

I'M AMAZED THAT I AGREED TO GET INVOLVED IN THE thing. There was Keith with this harebrained idea of a phantom girl dancing outside the first-floor washroom, or whatever, and there was me saying I'd help. One of us was definitely gonzo, but both of us were showing symptoms.

I got hold of Jill Hawes on the phone, flattered her so much that I thought I might barf into the receiver, and finally got her to agree to model. Then I made up a set of sketches, with locations, so that we'd have some idea what we were doing. I knew enough about ballet to know the kinds of things Jill should do with her body and enough about the school to know where she should do it.

Besides, at some level I sort of liked Keith.

Now I realize that doesn't relate. But so what? Mrs. Morris keeps on saying that my essays have to be organized. But life isn't organized. Life is a collection of random events held together by irony. So there.

And yes, I will get back to the story.

The three of us met at school the next Saturday morning. Keith had photo equipment and extension cords draped over his neck and arms so he looked like some electrician running amok. Jill was impatient to get going, as if *her* minutes were somehow worth more than *our* minutes. Of course, she could get away with that kind of crap because she was gorgeous. And I say this matter-of-factly, not because I'm jealous. It doesn't bother me that I've never been gorgeous. Only in weak moments—say when I'm spending Saturday night alone watching *Love Boat* on TV—have I ever *wanted* to be gorgeous.

Still, the fact that Jill was so absolutely, physically perfect always got her noticed. When she took off her heavy sweater, Keith couldn't unglue his eyeballs from the white leotards she wore underneath. I frankly thought the outfit was a bit tacky. She should at least have worn a bra.

"Keith, would you stop salivating for a second and look at these," I told him. "I've sketched out the whole thing on the clipboard here. Jill should be dancing through the photographs like Martha Graham or somebody like that."

"Oh, I *love* modern dance," Jill cooed. She was doing a limbering up exercise that kept drawing Keith's attention away from the outline. "Did you ever see Merce Cunningham when they were on TV?"

"I must have missed that," Keith said. He was acting like a toad.

"Too bad," she said, cutting him down soon enough.

Keith looked vaguely wounded.

"Stop acting like a Piggie, Keith. You might as well take style lessons from Frank Pescatore," I said.

"Huh?"

"Oh, never mind. Look, I think we should start at the front door and gradually move each shot up until we get to the roof. Then Jill disappears like the phantom she's supposed to be. Okay?"

"Looks good on paper. Make sure I do every shot twice just in case the first one doesn't work." Keith was getting down to business.

"Anything, so long as we don't have to do all this again," I told him.

I was not in a good mood. It also seemed to me that Jill Hawes was the most detestable twit I'd ever met. The way she reduced Keith's brain to marmalade upset me far more than it had any right to. At the time, I couldn't recognize my feelings as anything so simple as jealousy.

We were a pretty strange-looking crew as we made our way through the school. Luckily we were the only ones in the place besides the school janitor. He stared at us while Keith and I set up the first shot. Jill was supposed to appear at the end of this one, kind of a blur, like she was running away. Keith had to take two exposures—one of the hallway and its arches, the other of Jill disappearing.

"Let's try a run-through before I shoot it," Keith said, sensibly enough.

I counted down, Jill danced fleetingly, Keith pretended to press the cable release. The janitor watched all this with an obnoxious grin inspired, I'm sure, by Jill's leotards. I decided to ignore him.

"Okay, let's do it for real," I said. "Ready, three,

two, one." Jill danced, I held up the photoflood, Keith squeezed the cable release.

"That's one," Keith said.

"Okay, let's do it again."

Keith reshot the background while the janitor shook his head and walked away. I don't think this was a comment on our picture taking. It probably had more to do with the big sweater Jill put back on between shots.

When Keith was finished, Jill went back to her original position and waited for my count. Then she danced across the marble hall, more graceful this time, and Keith squeezed the release.

"Perfect," I said.

My mood improved with each picture we took. The various shots took us along the first-floor corridor, into the gym, and up to the science labs. I kept things moving and organized, Keith eventually got used to Jill so that he could look through his viewfinder without breathing hard, and Jill danced. As far as I could figure out, Jill couldn't do anything but dance. No, scratch that, she could also gorgeous. I realize that gorgeous is not normally a verb, but if anybody could gorgeous, then Jill could gorgeous.

When I went down to phone for a pizza, poor Keith was being gorgeoused. I felt sorry for him, leaving him alone with her, knowing that he'd be totally embarrassed in her presence. Personally, I think Keith's awkwardness is one of his more charming qualities. Nobody else thinks so, and certainly not Keith himself, but I do.

Then the pizza arrived and we ate. Keith dropped a pepperoni on his crotch and was embarrassed; Jill ate small portions and never even got tomato sauce on her lips; I pigged out.

"Keith," I said, "I've been thinking about the ending of this thing, you know, where Jill disappears. It doesn't make much sense to me. I mean, so far the camera's been chasing her around the school, so when she disappears, what does it mean? The girl never existed? It was all a dream?"

Jill looked at Keith with eyes like a fawn. Keith looked down where the pepperoni had stained his paints. Obviously he was at a loss for words.

"So here's my idea," I went on. "At some point, probably up on the roof, you come out from behind the camera and try to embrace the dream. You know, boy gets girl. But when you try to reach out for this phantom girl, she disappears. Do you see it?"

"Oh, I like that," Jill said.

"Well," Keith mumbled.

"It's like the impossibility of making dreams real. You can't step out of real life and touch the dream without destroying it."

"Oh, wow," Jill said.

"Yeah, well what do *you* think?" I asked, staring at Keith.

"Who's going to be the male model?" he asked.

"You."

"Me?"

"You."

"Who's going to take the pictures?"

"I will," I said.

"You?" Now it was Keith's turn.

"Me. I've used my father's Leica a hundred times."

"I didn't know your father had a Leica."

"There's lots of things you don't know about me, Keith. I'll make you a list sometime. But what about the idea? Do you like it?"

"Yeah," he said, smiling. "I like it."

We had to take three more shots before the final one, and these went quickly enough. Then we finally made it to the last shot and the last location—the roof. I unlocked the door to the supply room and Keith pushed open the door leading outside.

"I'm going to freeze," Jill whined, folding her arms.

I hoped she would, but I couldn't say that. "I'll get your coat and you can wear it until the last minute, okay? We're almost done."

"I just don't want to catch pneumonia."

Neither did I, so I got all our coats from the yearbook office.

"Okay," I said, taking over, "I want Keith in silhouette reaching out towards you, Jill, over there. Keep your coat on while I check the framing."

I peered through the viewfinder, organizing the shot so Keith's shaking hand would be reaching out, groping towards Jill.

"Now mark your positions, then get rid of your coat, Jill, and back into the pose. Ready? Go," I said.

Jill scrambled over to the doorway, discarded her coat, and reappeared in the viewfinder as a phantom dancer fleeing from the dark satyr. I realize that Keith is not normally much of a satyr, but in silhouette he filled the bill. Maybe it was a whole new side of him, one I hadn't noticed before.

"Great. One shot is enough," I shouted. "Jill, get your coat on and get out of the picture. Keith, freeze."

"I'm freezing already."

"Good. The last shot has you standing there. Now turn a little towards the spot where Jill was. Okay, that's perfect."

"My feet," Jill cried. "My feet are like ice."

"Great artists are supposed to suffer," I told her.

"Right now I'd rather just get warm," Keith said.

So the three of us retreated to the coffee machine on the first floor and we slurped the coffee down in a hurry. Jill's ride was out in the parking lot, but the guy didn't even offer to take us home. Talk about snotty! Keith and I had to walk.

Keith wanted to know what I thought about the shooting session and I said I'd know when I saw the photos. He wanted to know what I thought about Jill and I told him. I think the list of adjectives lasted me a good fifteen minutes.

"And what's a Piggie?" he asked, just before I turned off to go to Golden Voice's apartment.

"Huh?"

"A Piggie," he repeated. "That's what you called me."

"It's a male chauvinist pig. Everybody knows that. It's any guy who can only think about a woman in terms of her body. Somebody like the janitor or Frank."

"Am I a Piggie?" he asked.

"Sometimes you act like one. Sometimes you looked at Jill today like a Piggie—you know, lots of hopeless lust, all talk, no boom boom. But mostly you're not. You're an Iggie."

"An Iggie?"

"Yeah, an ignoramus. You're really pretty clueless, Keith. No offense. You don't know if you should drool over it, or go for it, or back away and become a monk. Still, there could be worse things."

"Like?"

"Like a Pervie. The flasher would be a Pervie, for instance, or that guy who tried to rape Gracie Ratinski."

"But what about the nice guys?" he asked.

"Show me one."

"Your boyfriend?"

"Oh," I said, forgetting for a second about the grad student I had made up. I had a flash of panic when I thought Keith had found out about Weyman. It was hard to tell. Maybe someone had blabbed about it. But I decided to play dumb and keep up my story of the grad student. "That whole thing isn't working out," I said. "I think I'm going to ditch him over Christmas."

"How come?" Keith asked.

"Because I can't come up with a label for him."

Keith laughed and I said goodbye before I got tangled up any further in my lies. I wondered, afterward, what I was trying to hide from him. Was I trying to lead Keith on, or worse still, was I becoming a tease? Or maybe—and this was really gonzo—maybe I was starting to like Keith, to *really* like Keith.

Chapter 13

KEITH

My mother, father, and I had a chance to see God over the Christmas holidays. The three of us were each bearing a gift for Steven, though we couldn't quite come up with gold, frankincense, and myrrh. My mother bought him a new sport jacket from Gordon's, essentially similar to the one she had given me, except that Steven's fit properly. My father wrapped up a package of twelve paperback novels on various topics—from a William Styron novel to a book on Toyota maintenance. My father's gift to me had been full of sci-fi novels, only four of which I had already read.

My gift was really for Steven and Sandra both. It was a small portfolio of photographs I had taken of Melissa, their three-year-old. Sandra was quite enthusiastic about the gift. Steven gave it about as much attention as he usually gave to Melissa herself, which wasn't much.

I had funny, mixed feelings about spending the Christmas vacation in Ann Arbor. Basically, we mortals are never very comfortable in the presence of God. Moses didn't look forward to going up the mountain and Paul must have really panicked when God snuck up on him along the road to Damascus.

I hadn't been comfortable with Steven since my brother ascended to god status sometime during high school. That's when it became apparent that he had some sort of gift. It wasn't just intelligence, though his was certainly high enough, but more a special kind of touch. When Steven picked up a tennis racket, in five minutes he knew how to play and in a season was contending for the league championship. When he took on the yearbook, it immediately expanded from a 96-page black-and-white picture book to a 144-page extravaganza with color pages and outrageous articles on student life. When Steven graduated from Wagnalls, he picked up almost every award the school had to give.

I suppose it was just as well that Steven didn't go to Harvard where he would have been just one more god in a pantheon. At Ann Arbor, he stood out. He was on student government in a year, chairman of the President's advisory board in two, and rumored to be running soon for City Council even though he still hadn't graduated. His academic work slid somewhat, but he was so well liked in the biology department that he got an interesting lab job while students with higher marks were still cleaning tables at the cafeteria. Somehow things always seemed to work out for Steven. That's what I admire about him; that's also what I envy.

My parents visited Ann Arbor for only a day, spending the night in a hotel before they left on a short vacation. I knew why they never slept over at Steven's apartment. It was because the dirt and clutter drove my orderly father crazy. Dishes were falling out of the kitchen cabinets, the baby's toys were strewn everywhere, and a line of dirt and fingerprints ran along each wall at exactly Melissa's height. My mother tried hard to avoid commenting on the mess, but finally she "just had to say something." Sandra looked at the ceiling while this was going on and I felt embarrassed for both of them. As far as I was concerned, my bed in the fold-out sofa was just fine after I brushed away the cookie crumbs.

Though Steven and I spent over a week in the apartment, more or less together, we had little contact. He was always busy with something: his job, a term paper, committee meetings. Steven had never been a very introspective person, but any traces of that had disappeared entirely. What remained was the fantastic energy he showed in confronting every task in front of him, from defending rent controls to finishing a paper on Marx's analysis of religion.

All I really wanted from Steven was a chance to show him the photo series I had done at the school. I had brought the prints with me just for that, even rushing the darkroom work to get it done in time. I wanted to show them to Steven before I showed them to Jane, because . . . well, I wasn't sure why. For some reason it still seemed very important to get Steven's approval. At least it was important enough to collar Steven alone one night, just before he rushed off to a meeting.

"Okay, Keith, what do you want?" Steven asked me as I drew him aside. Sandra was looking after the baby in the living room, so we had the bedroom to ourselves.

"I want to show you something," I said.

"Any time, Keith, but right now—"

"It won't take long. Here—look at these," I told him, handing him the bundle of unmounted prints.

God stepped off the mountain for a minute to look at the pictures, slowly at first, then faster as he got towards the end of the series.

"Pretty girl," he said when he was finished. "Looks like you're finally doing all right for yourself."

I was stunned. I don't know what I expected Steven to say, but somehow that comment cut me right down. It was as if he had made trivial everything I was trying to do.

"She's not my girlfriend, just a model. This is going to be the opening spread for the yearbook."

"That should really blow Wagnalls right over."

"Yeah, but what do you think? You think they're good?" I asked, trying to prompt him.

"I think they'll cause a sensation. Maybe get you tossed right out of school. Look, someday when I have more time, I'll give you advice on what to say when the administration hauls you down to the office over these, but right now I've got to get going."

"I know, but—"

"So I'll talk to you about it tomorrow, okay?"

"Okay," I said, though that was a lie. Tomorrow was not okay. Even right now was not okay. I felt as if Steven had just added several light-years to the distance between us.

Steven and I didn't talk that next day or the day after, at least not about the photographs. They seemed to have slipped from his consciousness altogether and I was reluctant to bring them up again. It wasn't as if Steven hadn't looked at them, the problem was that he hadn't *seen* them.

I spent the rest of the vacation sitting around the apartment, playing with Melissa, reading sci-fi novels, and feeling like I had been sent into limbo. The time wasn't unpleasant, it just didn't have any meaning. I had brought my camera with me, but I couldn't even find the energy to go out and shoot some pictures.

The only person I could really talk to, besides Melissa whose vocabulary was somewhat limited, was Sandra. I had always liked and trusted her more than any other adult, except perhaps my father. She had a quietness that made sense to me.

On the day I was to leave for home, I was sitting in the kitchen with Sandra and drinking one last cup of coffee before the bus trip. Melissa was off at the daycare center and Sandra had taken the morning off from her library job at the university to drive me to the bus depot.

"Did you take any pictures while you were here?" she asked.

"I was going to," I said, "but I never quite got around to it."

"I'm like that, too. I don't get around to things, somehow. You did such a wonderful job on those photographs of Melissa that I thought you might be shooting something more serious."

"Sometimes I do. I'm a regular Ansel Adams," I said, making fun of myself for no good reason.

"Well, that's good, Keith. Your photographs are technically excellent, but what you need to become an

Ansel Adams is to develop your own eye. You have to start seeing the world your own way, which probably wouldn't be the same way Ansel Adams saw it."

"We're a little short on mountains and deserts."

"That's not what I mean."

Of course it wasn't. I had thought about the problem often enough, the problem of working out my own style, somehow putting my own stamp on the photographs I took. But I wasn't there yet; I wasn't ready. Even when I did the photo series for the yearbook, I had borrowed the idea and just adapted it for my own needs. At some point, I was sure, I could move beyond borrowing. But what I had was still good, still worth more attention than Steven had given it.

"I just finished a photo sequence for the yearbook," I blurted out.

"What's it like?"

"Well, it's kind of a fantasy sequence using the school as a backdrop with the phantom image of a girl superimposed—"

"Hey, go a little slower," Sandra said.

"Well, trying to talk about it is dumb," I told her. "I've got the photos here in the suitcase if you'd like to see them."

"Are they good?" she asked.

I was surprised by how quickly I answered. "Yeah, they're good."

I pulled the envelope of prints from my suitcase and handed them to Sandra. It seemed to me that I was very nervous without any particular reason to be nervous. The series *was* good, even if it hadn't impressed Steven, even if Jane and I were the only people who would ever understand it.

Sandra went through the pictures more slowly than Steven had. She often smiled, responding to something in one print or another. When she finished, her verdict was quick. "Dynamite."

"What?"

"Dynamite. This series is really strong, Keith. It's much too good for the old Wagnalls yearbook. You should do a show."

"Well, really . . ."

"No, I mean it. I know something about photography, so I can see the quality here. This series is better than some of the prints I've been buying for the university collection. The whole concept is very, very sophisticated. Especially at the end, where the photographer tries to reach out and touch the dream."

"Well, I had some help on that," I admitted.

"I guess you had to. But this is *your* work, Keith. It's really quite a personal statement, I think. But what does it have to do with a high school yearbook?"

"The theme is 'Personal Growth.' "

"You're kidding."

I shook my head.

"Thinking back, I can believe it. Mrs. Morris is still the advisor, right? It sounds just like her."

"We're going to switch in a new text for her Wordsworth poems. We've got something by Ferlinghetti and quotes from Doug and the Slugs and groups like that."

Sandra began to laugh. "She'll have a fit. I can see all two hundred pounds of her turning beet red when this comes out."

"I could get in real trouble," I said, smiling with her.

"Trouble with Mrs. Morris you can probably handle," Sandra told me. "But I'm serious about your doing a show, Keith. I know the people who run a photography gallery here and they might give you wall space. I could even buy a print for the university out of the show."

"But the prints aren't *that* good. I'd have to correct the exposures and clean them up . . ."

"Sure, sure. But when you get that done, send me a set and I'll see what I can arrange. Don't make up the big prints until we get a commitment from the gallery. Just send me something to give them an idea."

"Well, sure," I said, overwhelmed by all this. No one had ever taken my photography that seriously and now—a gallery show?

"I didn't even know you were doing work like this," she said, almost as if she were looking at me in a new way.

"It's only been the last three years."

"I guess it's my fault, Keith. I've always seen you as the kid brother, as if you didn't even have your own life. After all, you were only twelve or thirteen when Steven and I started living together, so I guess I didn't pay much attention."

"I was stuck in the shadow," I said. It was Jane who had first used those words, trying to figure me out. And I knew right away that the image was a good one.

"How's that?"

"Steven always managed to get all the light, so I ended up standing in his shadow. It's only since he's been away that I . . ."

"Right," she agreed. "I can see that. We both have the same problem, really, and I like the way you phrase it. Of course Steven has to have the light. He couldn't survive without everybody admiring him all the time."

"Yeah, but it makes it harder for us," I said.

"It wouldn't be so bad if Steven would pay a little more attention to those of us stuck here in the dark."

"Well, he's always so busy with important things," I said, sticking up for him.

"That's just your hero-worship, Keith. It's easy to think that everything Steven does is important because that's what he wants you to think. Then there's the other side. You tend to overlook the screw-ups and the failures. I can't." Sandra was looking at the tablecloth, perhaps filling in her words with memories.

"But you have to admit that Steven gets things done," I said. "It's easy to criticize him because maybe he spreads himself too thin. But when it comes to taking action, well, there he is." I was sounding like my mother.

"But if you look behind the causes and the politics," Sandra began, "you find somebody who's really superficial and doesn't have the strength to admit it. Look behind all his political buddies and the women—all the women—and you find somebody who hasn't got any friends. Only admirers."

"But Steven's a success."

"At what cost?" Sandra shot back. "The superstar is almost flunking out because he's so busy with committee reports and research groups and meetings of the something-or-other society. He hasn't got time for school. Or his family."

Sandra wasn't looking at me any more. I wasn't even sure whether she was talking to me or using me to explore her own thoughts.

"So Steven's family takes second or third place," Sandra went on. "Melissa's growing up and he hardly has time for her. And he seems to have time for lots of women, but never for his wife." Sandra was upset. Her hands trembled on the table.

I didn't know what to say.

"Keith," she said, "if you talk to him, maybe you could tell him that his family is tired of living in a shadow. We need some of the light ourselves. And we'd like a real father and a real husband for a change." She was fighting hard to keep control, holding back the tears through sheer power of will.

I was embarrassed. "I can't talk to him any more," I said.

"Somebody's got to."

Conversation stopped. I wanted to look away, at my feet, anywhere. I'm not good with people, with emotions. Too much like my father.

"Oh, it's time," Sandra said, suddenly snapped back to the immediate world. She smiled at me, almost by way of apology for everything she had dumped out, then looked a little embarrassed. She grabbed a Kleenex from the box on the kitchen shelf before we left for the bus depot.

Riding back on the bus, I thought about Sandra and her sudden show of emotion. There was something wrong in Ann Arbor, maybe something even Steven didn't know about yet. And there was something right going on in my life, maybe something that would get me out of the shadows and into some light of my own.

Chapter 14

JANE

Noel, noel, noel,
May all Jane's enemies go to hell.

THERE'S SOMETHING PHONEY ABOUT THE WHOLE Christmas season. I mean, here you are in the middle of winter with nothing to do unless you like freezing your buns off on some mountaintop with a pair of pricey 1 x 4's on your feet, and you're supposed to be merry? It's no wonder the Druids invented a midwinter holiday. Otherwise everyone would commit suicide between November and March.

My father and I went through the pretense of Christmas cheer. He bought me a Sony Walkman radio, probably so I could listen to his show between classes at school. The thing I like about the radio is its built-in microphone. When somebody wants to talk to you they have to speak into the mike, otherwise you won't hear them over the music. I figure it'll drive my father gonzo.

Keith went to Ann Arbor to see his brother. He calls his brother God when he's feeling depressed, but that reveals a lot about their relationship. Imagine having God as your brother! Talk about feeling inferior! I tried to explain to Keith that we both live in shadows. He's always eclipsed by his brother, I'm always having to push my father out of the limelight. In Keith's case, I think he's making some progress in getting his share of the light. In my case, well, I'm trying.

I think my mother wanted to see me over Christmas. At least that's what Golden Voice told me. Well, fat chance, lady. Not after what you did to me—and I don't care how sorry you are now or how rough it was then.

So I stayed in the boonies through the holidays. On Christmas Day my father revealed that he'd been quietly working on a serious replacement for his now-divorced wife. I think I arched my eyebrows in response. Three months and he thinks it's serious? You'd think the old man had the emotional maturity of a fifteen-year-old.

Anyway, Golden Voice made arrangements over Christmas for me to meet his latest woman, a thirty-five-year-old sales rep named Audrey. I wish he'd pick them a little bit older, say some nice fifty-year-old biddie, but he goes for the young ones. Someday his women will be younger than I am. Right now, they fall into the older sister category. And I *never* wanted an older sister.

Still, I try to be open-minded. I recognize Oedipal jealousy when I see it in the mirror. I fight it and try to be nice. But it never seems to work out.

My father decided that the three of us would get

together at a restaurant. I think he liked the semipublic meeting area because he thought it would keep me under control. Once, when I was thirteen, he brought one home for dinner and I threw a plate at her. No, that's an exaggeration. I dropped a plate on the floor while I was thinking about throwing it at her. But it's almost the same thing.

We went to a place called Eduardo's which is about as fancy as restaurants get around here. It's a steak house that has Muzak instead of a jukebox. Otherwise the place is pretty heavy on the arborite. We got to the restaurant first, of course, because my father likes to be a proper gentleman. I sat so I could see people coming into the place, wondering if I could pick Audrey out when she came in.

It was easy. My father always goes for the same types: blondes with big boobs, wide hips, and heavy makeup. Audrey was a little less blonde than some, a little slimmer than most, but her makeup was a dead giveaway, a Max Factor extravaganza.

"Hello, Audrey," my father said. The basso profundo was as liquid as honey. It's no wonder they fall for him.

"Hi, Tom," she replied. "Jane, I'm Audrey."

"Yeah." I tried to smile. I sent signals to the muscles controlling the corners of my mouth, but a smile doesn't come out quite right when you have to concentrate on it.

"Why don't we all have a drink," my father said affably. The waiter came over and they asked for some white wine. I ordered a Southern Comfort. Then they chitchatted about the snow. People do that up here.

"And how do you like your school, Jane?" Audrey asked.

"It'll do," I said.

My father shot me one of his looks. *The* look. He even cleared the golden throat, about to say something.

"I mean," I went on, heading off the tirade, "that it has possibilities. But it's pretty provincial."

"Isn't it ever!" she said. Audrey was from Chicago and thought of herself as an exile. She had followed her ex-husband out here, gotten a job at the radio station, ditched the husband but kept the job. For a few minutes, while she told me about all this, I almost liked her. Then things went downhill.

"I wouldn't want to be a kid in school today," she said.

"Why's that?" my father asked.

"Well, you know, Tom. Jane and her friends have to face things we never did: drugs, sex, and all. The pressure on them is really extreme. It's no wonder that so many of them get into trouble."

"I don't know many kids in trouble," I said. I was excluding myself.

"Well, you know what I mean."

"No, what do you mean?" I asked her. Why do I say these things?

"Kids today seem to have so many more problems than they used to. We never had drugs back in the fifties. If somebody asked me what marijuana was back in high school I would have guessed it was a Mexican resort."

She smiled. My father smiled.

"But you had alcohol," I said, with effort.

"Well, yes."

"Which is more destructive to the body and probably more dangerous to society than dope."

"I suppose."

"And for all the advantages of that wonderful time you had growing up, you haven't made the world any better for it. The economy is sick, the arms race gets worse, there's an actor straight out of B-movies sitting in the White House . . ."

"I didn't make the world," she said.

"That's right, Jane," my father joined in. "You can't pin responsibility for the state of the world on a single generation."

"Some people can't take responsibility at all," I said, staring right at him.

"Jane!" It was *the* voice with *the* look.

I went ahead anyway. "I just get tired of parents feeling sorry for kids. Me, I feel sorry for you. You had your chance to put the world back together better than it was and you blew it. Then you turn around and pity the poor kids who inherit the mess and tell yourselves how wonderful it was. Well, it makes me want to puke."

At this point, I felt like everyone in the restaurant was turning to stare at us.

Golden Voice was embarrassed. "I think that's enough, Jane."

"It's all right," Audrey said, trying to smooth things over.

"No it's not," I disagreed.

"I said that's enough," my father spat out between his teeth. He was all too aware that people were listening, so he grabbed my arm and gave it a pinch for emphasis.

"Let go of me," I hissed with a venom that was obvious to anyone listening in.

I pulled my arm out of his grip and stood up before he could do anything else. In a second I had escaped from the restaurant and made it to the cold air outside. It felt good.

After a while I realized that my father wasn't going to follow me outside. I also knew that I wasn't going back inside. So I stuck out my thumb and hitched a ride back to the apartment.

When I got home I noticed that my father's grip had left a bruise. And that was only my *first* bruise over Christmas.

I got the second one from Pete Weyman at a New Year's Eve party in Gracie Ratinski's basement. An intelligent person would immediately ask two questions about this. First, why would I go to a party at Gracie Ratinski's, much less her rather tacky basement? The answer to that one is relatively simple. I went because the alternative was staring at the idiots in Times Square on the boob tube at home. As it turned out, all I did was stare at the idiots in Times Square on a projection TV.

This leads to the second question, why did I go out with Pete again? After our rather dismal first date and my refusal to see him again all through November, why did I give in and agree to go out to the party?

I haven't got a good answer. I could lie and say I was lonely, or horny, or ready to spite my father, or anxious to prove my status, but those aren't the real reasons I went out with Pete. The real reason is that I'm screwed up in the head.

The party was pretty dismal. It consisted of two hundred stale records from somebody's sister's cousin, a fair amount of booze stolen from various rec rooms, two bottles of champagne for maybe thirty people, and some homegrown grass. If I remember accurately, at the stroke of midnight Pete was looking on jealously while I toasted the new year with Brad Price. Brad was telling me something vaguely amusing about a dance at his brother's house. I was smiling as best I could while lighting up one more cigarette. Brad seemed to misinterpret the smile and move in a little closer. And Pete came storming over. He pulled Brad out of the way and proceeded to announce in a slurred voice, "You're supposed to be with me."

"Huh?" I was not in top form at the time.

"You're supposed to be over here with me, not with Price. I've been looking for you," he said accusingly.

"So you found me."

"Well, I don't want you going around with him."

"I was just talking."

"Well, don't do it. I just don't want you playing around with anybody else."

"I'll do what I goddamn want and play around with anybody I please!" I snapped back.

Pete's face very quickly became red with anger. And he punched me—a real sock—no playing around. My arm stung like I'd burned it on a kettle.

Naturally, I slugged Pete back. Once. In the eye. Pete fell over backwards on the floor, more from surprise and drunkenness than from me. By the time he got even halfway up, the whole party had gathered around him. Pete stomped off, disgraced for life.

Somebody gave me a ride home after that, around three in the morning. When I got into the apartment, I saw my father asleep on the couch. He'd been waiting up for me, like he always did.

I watched him breathing, sound asleep, and felt a little sad. Maybe it was because I was tired and drunk, but I suddenly saw the two of us as the same person, all tough and armored on the outside, trying to protect the more fragile person within. For a second, I wanted to give him a kiss to show him something that I couldn't bring myself to say out loud, but the phone rang before I did.

It was Pete, wanting to apologize. I unplugged the phone before he could get into it, but the noise had already awakened my father.

"Who was it?" he asked, rubbing the sleep from his eyes.

"Just some jerk," I said, walking over to the couch. Golden Voice was sitting up now, awake, and I tried to feel the same way about him that I had a moment ago. But it wouldn't work—the feeling wouldn't come back.

Chapter 15

KEITH

JANE DIDN'T TELL ME ABOUT WEYMAN—FRANK DID. Of course, by January it was all over school. Jane Flemming, the mouthy girl from New York, had punched out Wagnalls' resident male heartthrob.

"Well, don't take a fit, Keith," Frank said, apparently in response to the look on my face.

"I couldn't care less," I said.

"Yeah, sure. Sure. The only reason I said anything is 'cause everybody else already knows, so you might as well, if you know what I mean. I betcha he's gettin' a little you know what."

"F— off," I told him. I stomped away, angry and frustrated, embarrassed at my own swearing.

It was my first day back after the Christmas break. The photo series was in my gym bag, and a certain amount of confidence, thanks to Sandra, had swollen my head. The news about Weyman immediately brought my head back to its normal size. Of course I told myself that I had no claim on Jane. I told myself that there was no reason her going out with Weyman should affect me at all. We were friends and friendship is not exclusive. Jane had never said that she *wasn't* going out with a guy from Wagnalls.

On the other hand, she never said that she *was*. Is that deception? Is it lying if a person merely leaves out certain key items of information? Sure it is.

So I sat through English and math as depressed as I have ever been. I was blaming myself, reminding myself—just like I always used to—that I was insignificant, unworthy, and second-rate. But then that feeling passed. I guess I was losing my ability to wallow in self-pity and was developing something new—anger. The more I thought about it, the angrier I became. I wouldn't have expected her to turn Pete Weyman down—nobody ever turned him down—but at least she could have told me about it. She just made it worse by hiding the fact. If I were her friend, pure and simple, she should have no reason to cover it up.

"Keith."

I was standing at my locker at the end of the day when I heard Jane's voice. I didn't turn around.

"Keith," she said again, walking up to me. I couldn't ignore her this time.

"What do you want?"

"Jeez, nice mood. Look, you were going to show me the pictures today. Remember?"

"Yeah, but—"

"No buts. I want to see them so I can get started on the layout. So come on."

She's like that: bossy, demanding, insensitive to other people. As we walked to her place, I mentally listed everything wrong with Jane's personality. She's a tease and a manipulator; she's opinionated without the brains to back up her ideas; she's vain but pretends not to be; and she's so screwed up she doesn't know where the screw-up ends and the real Jane begins. She's not even *that* good-looking.

"Keith, what's eating you?" she asked. We had reached her apartment and I was taking off my coat.

"Nothing."

"Oh, sure. Did God give you a hard time in Ann Arbor?" She looked at me with those big eyes, full of concern.

"God's in trouble. He can't seem to balance school and family and all the causes he wants to fight for."

"That's real progress, Keith. It's the first time I've ever heard you admit that Steven is less than perfect. Maybe you're starting to see him as he really is. Demystification!"

"Cut the psychology, will you?"

"It's just a way of getting at the truth," she said.

"The truth! What do you care about the truth?" I was getting angry all over again.

"What's that crack supposed to mean?" she asked.

"If you want to talk about the truth, why don't you start with Pete Weyman?"

Jane opened her mouth as if she wanted to say something, but no words came out. She stood there, looking at me, then turned away. Her face was red.

"I was going to tell you."

"When?" I just stared at her.

Jane couldn't look at me. I thought for a minute that she was trying to find a comeback, maybe something about her rights or her privacy. But I was wrong. Jane ran off to the living room, covering her face with her hands.

I stood in the hall, wondering what to do. The anger had blown out and I felt lousy. I saw Jane in the living room with her head bowed, her breathing uneven and raspy. I knew it wouldn't be fair to walk out.

I went in and sat on a chair across from her. I wanted to put my arms around her and say that it was all right. But I couldn't; and it wasn't.

Gradually she got control back. "I'm sorry," she said.

"Me too."

"I was going to tell you. I kept on saying to myself that I had to tell you, but I couldn't. . . . I don't even know why."

"It would have been better."

"How'd you find out?"

"From Frank."

"Oh no," she said. "I can imagine the stories that he told you."

"I cut him off before he could start," I told her.

"None of it's true. I know what the Yahoos at school are saying, but it's not true."

"So what is the truth?"

"Oh, I don't know, Keith. It's not that I even like him that much, but I got tired of sitting around here and he kept on asking me out. I couldn't very well go out alone."

I almost said that she could have gone out with me, but I didn't have to. She read my mind.

"And you're a friend, Keith. Really, you're my only friend here. I just couldn't risk you, you know? A boyfriend with me lasts for maybe a couple months and then, zap, it's over. I didn't want that to happen to us."

"Yeah," I said, though I didn't like that explanation much.

"So that's it," she said.

"No, that's not it. Why didn't you tell me?"

"Because you're too sensitive and I knew you'd take it the wrong way. He's got nothing to do with us."

"But you were covering it up since November. And I'm walking around like Dopey when everybody else in the school seems to know about it. That's not fair, Jane."

"I know. I'm going to stop." She was getting upset again. "It's because I'm such an awful liar, Keith. It's something inside me. I can't take the real world so I cover up everything with lies. I can't help it."

"We all do that."

"Not the way I do. I'm sick, Keith. Do you remember the penthouse?"

"What penthouse?"

"The first time you walked me home I told you I lived in the penthouse. I thought for sure you'd remember when you finally came up here. I was so afraid that you'd see through me. People always do. I used to tell the kids in New York that my mother was violent and that she had to be kept in a straightjacket all the time. I even made up these incredible letters from her . . . because for the longest time she never sent me any real letters. I couldn't admit the simple truth to the rest of them, that she just walked out on my father and me. I couldn't admit the truth because it hurt too much."

"But kids do that kind of thing," I said, trying to reassure her.

"Kids!" she cried. "I *still* do it!" Her eyes were blazing now. "I can't even tell the truth to you, the only friend I have. I still have to hide behind lies because I'm afraid to come out into the real world."

"Hey, it's all right."

"No, it's not! Keith, please listen to me." She was clutching her knees tightly in her arms. "Remember the first time you walked me home. I told you my mother was dead. Remember? And later on I told you that was just the way I thought of her, but then, then it was another lie. And Keith, I'm still a liar. You know that Leica I said my father owned? There's no Leica. There's nothing but a stupid Instamatic. And you know that boyfriend I told you about, the twenty-four-year-old grad student? He never existed. He's a figment of my imagination, Keith. I've never had a real boyfriend, not even in New York. I'm afraid to. I guess that's why I lied to you."

Jane was crying now. I went over to her and cradled her in my arms as if she were a small child and a simple hug might take away the hurt.

"I'm sorry, really," she said, blubbering. "I just didn't know how to handle you. You wanted to get close to me, and I didn't know how to deal with that so I made up this guy." She stopped talking and sniffed. "It's not that I didn't like you, it isn't that, it's just . . . oh, it's just that I'm so screwed up."

Jane cried harder and this time I did more than hold her. I leaned forward and began kissing her cheeks. When Jane tried to talk, I kissed her again, this time on the lips. The second kiss was more than just "friends."

"Don't do that," she told me.

"Why not?" I asked.

"Because I don't know what to do about you and you're making me all confused."

Her big eyes were looking up into mine and I wanted to kiss her again. All the rules that went with being friends were useless now. I wanted a whole new set of rules, but Jane wasn't ready.

"Not now, Keith," she said, pulling away from me. "Maybe not ever. Don't make all this harder on me than it already is. My life is all messed up right now and I've got to sort it out. Besides, I don't want to lead you on because . . . Listen, I already told Pete that I'd go with him to the big end-of-semester party."

"With Pete? To Nancy Suddaby's?" The Suddaby party was famous as the closest thing to an orgy that we ever had in our town.

"Yeah." Jane stood up and got a cigarette out of her purse. "He apologized about the New Year's thing so I said okay. I feel so stupid now."

I didn't know what to say.

"Why don't you get a date and come too?" Jane was getting back in control of herself now.

"Who?"

"Ask Jill," Jane suggested. "She thinks you're cute and you can always bribe her with a picture."

"She wouldn't go out with me."

"Why not? Everybody else is afraid to ask her out. That's what she told me. Besides, Keith, you're a lot more attractive than you think you are."

"Yeah?" I wanted to hear it again.

"You've got a lot to offer. You're smart and interesting, talented, with not a bad bod. I think she was really impressed with you when we shot the photo series."

"Really?"

"Really. Now can we stop all this?" she said, drying her eyes. The other Jane was in control, all tough and hard and serious. The Jane that I had seen before, the one that was hurt and scared, got pushed back inside her. "I want to see the photo series, Keith," she said. Her voice was calmer now. Strong. Just like always.

"Sure," I said, handing the pictures over. "You know, maybe I will call Jill. The worst she can do is say no."

Jane looked up at me.

"And besides, it'd give me a chance to get even." I laughed and shook my head. I was starting to sound like Jane.

Chapter 16

JANE

WHY DO I ALWAYS SCREW THINGS UP FOR MYSELF?

I didn't *really* want Keith to go out with Jill. She's nothing but a dumb blonde without the brains to fill even a moderate-size thimble. And Keith deserves better than that. But I hadn't expected Jill to say yes. You'd think somebody as gorgeous as that would have been booked for Suddaby's party since age three, like an arranged marriage. Who would have guessed that Keith would phone at the right time to fill a desperate void in her social life? Who knows—maybe she even liked Keith, just like she said.

And I was stuck with Weyman! I mean, there's only so much pawing and hickeys a person can ordinarily stand. But once Keith had his date arranged with Jill, there was no way I would back out on my date with Pete. I knew perfectly well why Keith wanted to get even with me, and I guess I could handle that. But if I ended up sitting home, he'd be on top. There was no way I'd let that happen. At least, not then. Besides, who wanted to watch more *Love Boat* reruns while everybody else went to Suddaby's party?

The idea behind the party was to fight back against the winter right in the middle of it—summer in January. The heat in the house would be turned way up, the hot tub bubbling away, and everybody would dress as if they were on the beach at Fort Lauderdale.

All this became possible because Nancy's parents were *actually* in Florida and had left the house in her care, just as they had idiotically trusted her older sisters years before. I knew from the way Nancy and everyone else described previous parties that this one would be wild.

The evening of the party, my father was at work. It was a good thing he wasn't home to see Pete, who came to the door wearing a winter overcoat and a pair of boots. In between were a pair of very hairy legs.

"You look like the Riverdale Flasher," I said.

"Yeah," he grinned back at me. Taking the cue, Pete unbuttoned his coat and flashed his outfit—a tiny, tiny bathing suit and a Hawaiian lei. "Did you hear the news? They caught some guy who's supposed to be the flasher."

"Who'd they get? I bet it was Mr. Shank."

"Nah," Pete said. "Some pharmacist from the east end. How do I look?"

"Like an escapee from *Beach Blanket Bingo.*"

"Pretty good, huh?"

"Yeah," I said to humor him.

"Uh, watcha got under the clothes? I mean, what are you wearing at the party?"

"You'll see plenty when we get there," I told him.

When I first put on my bikini I had intended to throw

on a coat and go to the party as is. But the more I thought about it, the more I worried about how I'd look. I had put on five pounds over Christmas, so I was bulging out all over. I didn't mind teasing Pete a little, but I didn't feel like fighting him off in the car, either. Maybe that's why I put on a sweater and some jeans before he showed up.

"Everybody's coming to the party," Pete said, starting up the car.

"So I hear." I turned on the radio.

"Did you know that Jill Hawes is coming with Keith Hartman?"

"Really?" Can I ever sound dumb when I want to!

"Yeah. I tell you, that guy was a zero for a long time, but when he decides to go for it, he goes right for the best. Did you ever hear about his brother and the library teacher?"

"What about them?"

"Right on top of the Dewey decimal cards." The look on his face showed that he was imagining the scene in detail.

"I don't believe it."

"Ask anybody," Pete said.

We had to park halfway down the block from Nancy's house, one of the penalties for being fahionably late. I survived the trip through the snow banks well enough, but Pete kept complaining about his goosebumps. And no, I didn't want to see them. The only question in my mind was whether I could last through the party if I had to spend it in Pete's company.

Nancy Suddaby was at the door to let us in, dressed in a California swim outfit that probably cost more than my whole wardrobe. Pete unbuttoned his coat to do the flasher bit again. Nancy shrieked as if he were the real thing. Then she gave him a kiss which seemed to go beyond the hello-nice-to-see-you variety. Not that I *cared* much, but I *noticed*.

The house was a sprawling, ranch-style affair that seemed to have three or four different levels without ever making it to a real second floor. I was expecting paintings on black velvet and K-Mart couches with plastic covers. Instead I found Braque lithographs and furniture from Milan. Nancy's parents had taste. Since Nancy had none, I determined that she must have been adopted.

"The bar's at the back and the hot tub's to the left," Nancy said, very hostess-y.

"I brought Scotch," Pete announced.

"I'm just glad you brought *you*," she said, grinning.

I thought I was going to throw up.

"You want to take your clothes off here?" she asked me, implying the front hall.

"I think I'd rather use a bathroom," I said.

She shrugged and pointed down the hall. I went into the mirrored washroom and stripped down to my bikini. Then I checked out my reflection. Not Jill Hawes, maybe, but sexy enough.

"Fantastic," Pete drooled. My skin crawled as if he were feeling me up with his eyeballs. I folded my arms to frustrate him.

We went back to the bar where a bunch of Mint Juleps were lined up. By this time I was pretty thirsty from the overheated air of the house, so I finished my first drink in a minute or so. I think the thermostat must have been up around ninety because Pete was sweating like crazy. I don't sweat; I suffer. I thought they were carrying this Summer in January idea a bit far.

Most of the kids were down by the hot tub. The noise of both the crowd and the stereo got louder as we got closer. The room itself was packed. There must have been eighty people crowded from the glass wall at one end, past the deck and hot tub, over to the doorway. The hot tub was filled to overflowing with an assortment of bodies. I wanted to go in myself, but I wasn't sure about the group grope.

Looking around the place, I saw everyone but Keith. Frank was over in the corner, alone of course, busy ogling every girl in the room. Lou Russell, the yearbook editor, was standing against one wall with his arms folded as if he were somehow above all this foolishness. Gracie Ratinski was laughing while various guys tried to untie the top of her bathing suit. Gloria and Patty were dancing, maybe with each other. Some guy had fallen down in the corner, dead drunk already, and people were carefully stepping over him. A kid who called himself Acid Rain was running the stereo as if he were flying a Boeing 747. A few drips like little Charlie Fisher were holding up the walls. Everybody else was dancing or bumping or talking or laughing. I liked it all.

What I really wanted was a cigarette, but Keith had been making so much fun of me as a smokeaholic that I was trying to cut back. He convinced me that I should give my lungs a chance to take in some air that wasn't full of carcinogens. But it wasn't easy. I had to do something to keep my mind off smoking.

Weyman was the obvious solution. "Let's dance," I said to Pete. I liked the pounding of the music because it made the whole world blotto. And the dancing kept my brain from fantasizing about a smoke.

"Want to cool off in the tub?" Pete asked after a while.

"Yeah, but it's too crowded."

"Better now than later. Right now you can keep your bathing suit on."

"And later?"

Pete just grinned. It was one of those grins that had *Piggie* written all over it.

"We'd better get in right away," I told him.

"Sure. Later we can go back." He winked to punctuate this, but I pretended not to notice.

Pete ordered two of his football buddies out of the tub to make room for us, then we slid into the bubbling water. The tub itself was warm and relaxing, or at least it was relaxing until Pete decided to use the darkness of it as an excuse to paw at me.

"Cut it out," I said.

"Cut it out or what?" he asked.

"Or I'll knee you," I told him, seriously enough.

"Later, then," he said, taking his hand away.

I shook my head and got out of the tub. The idea of "later" with Pete was becoming dangerous.

I finally saw Keith while I was dripping water onto the cedar deck. He was over by the stereo near a crowd of guys. I figured that the center of male attention next to him had to be Jill Hawes.

Keith looked out-of-place, as always. No matter how hard he tries, his clothes look like he dressed to be somewhere else. For the party he was wearing a pair of too-long cutoff jeans, a Hawaiian shirt that looked like it belonged to his father, and a straw hat.

The outfit didn't quite make it, but the effort was cute. It was pure Keith.

I could tell by the look on his face that Keith was feeling awkward. He didn't know how to handle the blonde beauty queen he had asked out and didn't know what to do about the crowd of guys who kept butting in on his date.

When Jill finally broke free from her crowd of admirers, I could see what brought all the attention. She was wearing a one-piece maillot that was cut away to reveal more flesh than my bikini did. Of course, *her* flesh was perfect. Not a sag or a mole or a zit on her entire flawless body. Just looking at her next to Keith made me even more desperate for a smoke. I gave in and borrowed one from Patty Something-or-other, but the puffing didn't help much.

I can't remember precisely how the hours passed. There was a lot of dancing and a little talk. Somebody said that Frank's father was running for mayor and we talked about that for a while. From garbage on the steps of City Hall to garbage inside it. Amazing how things can change. Somebody else tried to untie the top of my bikini at one point, but I gave him a quick elbow in the ribs. A third somebody carried me off to the hot tub for a second dunking, but the trip and the splash were friendly enough. I was into another Mint Julep and didn't care an awful lot. By the time one o'clock rolled around I had downed far too many drinks—you know how you lose count—and didn't care much about Keith or Jill or Pete or anything.

I had just managed to beg another smoke from Patty Something-or-other when Pete came to find me.

"Come on over to the hot tub," he said.

"I don't want to go in again," I told him. Besides, I had just started my second cigarette in two weeks. I wanted to enjoy it.

"C'mon," he said, grabbing my arm.

I should probably have clobbered Pete right then, but I was still feeling a little mellow. I followed behind him right to the edge of the cedar deck. Then I stopped cold. There in the hot tub were most of the football team doing a locker-room-after-the-big-game routine. In the buff.

"Let's go in," Pete said.

"Dream on, buddy," I told him, yanking my arm away.

"Come on, Jane," he said, reaching around me. "Don't be a tease." His hands were busy trying to untie my bikini.

"Stop it," I said.

"C'mon," he told me, his hands still busy behind me.

"Pete—" I began, but I knew he wasn't about to stop. I knew perfectly well the only thing that Pete respected.

So I kneed him.

"Oof," was the only sound he made.

And then I pushed him across the deck and into the hot tub.

As Pete went splashing into the water, I heard cheering and applause from everybody at the edge. I looked around the room and smiled. I think everybody at school who had ever wanted to get even with Pete Weyman was on my side right then. It was one of those golden moments, even if it was a little sick, and I enjoyed it. For the first time ever, I realized that not everyone at Wagnalls was a Yahoo. Maybe the ones applauding me weren't quite as hopeless as I had thought. Maybe some of them even liked me, just a little.

But it wouldn't have been smart to spend too much time enjoying the applause. I decided to beat a quick retreat before Pete could recover and try to restore his honor, caveman style.

I went off to hide in the bedroom where I had left my clothes. I was tired and a little drunk, so after I got dressed I lay back on the bed and waited for the room to stop spinning. The ceiling was still revolving slowly when I heard the door open. I sat up fast, afraid that it might be Weyman, but the face that I finally focused on was much nicer than his. It was Keith's.

"What are we doing here?" Keith asked.

"Huh?" I still wasn't really with it. The air blowing through the open window had cleared my brain a little, but not enough.

"I mean," Keith said, "what are you doing here with that turkey while I'm here with a dumb-dumb beauty queen? It's stupid."

"You're drunk, Keith."

"So are you, but that's not the problem." Keith sounded so serious but he just looked funny. During the party he had lost his hat and shirt and then gone into the hot tub with his cutoffs on. He was dried out now but still looking disheveled.

"What's the problem, then? Where's Jill?"

"Gone. Some guy, I don't even know him. I just turned around and she said she's leaving with him."

"Oh, Keith," I said, sitting down next to him and taking his hand.

"I don't care. I don't care about her anyhow. I just came tonight because . . . well, I don't know. I thought maybe you'd see me differently." Keith was fidgety but he held tighter to my hand.

"I don't have to see you any other way, Keith. I like you as you are," I said, honestly. I was still in a fog, but that was the truth, the real truth.

"Then why do you go out with Weyman? Who are you trying to hurt? Me? Your father? Jane, I can't take this any more."

"Keith, I can't take the psychoan . . . Jeez, I can't even say it I'm so drunk."

"Come on, I'll take you home."

"I don't want to go home," I said. I was getting a really funny feeling, all warm and fuzzy, but not in my head. I realized something that I'd been hiding from for months. I'd been so busy playing around with lies and getting even that I'd missed the obvious. I'd missed what was really inside, what I really needed all along.

"So what do you want?" Keith asked.

"You," I said.

I pulled Keith close to me and kissed him, once, and again. Then we fell back on the bed and I could feel him on top of me. Why had I fought against it for so long? Why hadn't I been able to see that Keith was the one I wanted?

He kissed me harder and deeper, pressing himself against me. I didn't want him to stop. It wasn't just because I was drunk, it was because I was seeing things clearly for the first time.

"Jane, I—" he began, searching for words.

"I know," I told him. "I know how you feel. And it's the same for me."

We kissed again, pulling each other close, trying to climb inside one another. For a time, while he was holding me, nothing else in the world mattered.

But the world wasn't ready to leave us alone. There was a noise in the hall and I heard my name yelled out. I tried to pay no attention, but Keith pulled back a little, listening. In a second the door opened and Lou Russell stuck in his head.

"Jane?"

I rolled away from Keith and sat up on the bed. "Yeah."

"Jane," Lou said, "we've been trying to find you."

"Well, I've been right here—with Keith." I was proud of that, proud to tell him.

Lou didn't acknowledge it at all. His face was serious. "Somebody called about your father," he said. "He's been taken to the hospital."

"Oh, my—"

"They think it's a stroke," Lou said.

I couldn't even finish my words. Keith took me, put my coat over my shoulders, and led me to his car. I couldn't talk, I couldn't cry, I couldn't *feel* anything. It wasn't fair—I had just started to feel so much.

Chapter 17

KEITH

I COULD TELL THAT JANE WAS IN SHOCK. FOR ONE thing, she wasn't talking. For another, she kept twisting her hands together as though she were trying to wash them clean. I tried talking to her once or twice but got no response.

It was a good thing that Jane had put her clothes back on. We would have looked pretty strange coming into the hospital with her in a bikini. As it was, I was the only one who looked peculiar and I'm used to that.

"How long before we get there?" she asked.

We were stopped for a light. "Not long," I told her. I waited for a minute and then asked, "Are you all right?"

Silence. She wasn't all right. Neither was I. The fuzziness and buzz of the party were gone. Now there were only the glaring headlights coming at us and Jane rubbing her hands.

I parked the car in the hospital lot as close to the

admitting door as I could. Jane was already halfway up the sidewalk by the time I had locked up. I had to run to catch up with her and the cold air stung at my bare legs.

The hospital doors opened as we stepped on the rubber mat. Jane looked very pale under the fluorescent lights. I knew that I looked merely ridiculous. We walked up to a counter where a middle-aged woman was typing a form. The woman's red hair was piled high on her head and her glasses were held on by a chain. Her skin looked starched.

"Excuse me," I said.

The woman ignored me and continued typing.

"I want to see my father," Jane blurted out. Her voice didn't seem loud to me, but it got some attention.

The woman at the desk looked up, not at Jane, but at me. She studied my outfit for a minute and then pursed her mouth. A year ago I would have felt embarrassed and wanted to fade into a wall; now I just wanted to slug her.

"It's about *my* father," Jane told her. "Thomas Flemming."

I could feel Jane trembling, so I reached over and took her hand. That seemed to help.

"I'm afraid only the immediate family is permitted to see Mr. Flemming," she said icily. "We've asked everyone else to go home."

"I'm not a goddamn fan, lady. I'm his daughter. Now what room is he in?" Jane said, raising her voice.

I think the woman was upset by the swearing. She seemed to flinch, but only for a second. "I'll have to have some identification."

Jane's purse was at the party.

"Look," I said. "It's two in the morning and we had to rush to get here. I'll vouch for her," I said.

The woman looked at my bare legs and shook her head. "Only a driver's license or other valid form of identification is permitted."

Jane pulled her hand out of mine. "I want to see my father," she said, her voice cracking.

"I'm sorry," the woman said, though obviously she wasn't.

"There must be something we can do," I told her.

"If the family doctor gives an authorization you can go ahead," the woman said. "What is the name of your doctor?"

"We don't have a doctor," Jane said. "We've only been living here for seven months." Jane began crying and I put my arms around her.

"I want to see the doctor on duty, you witch," I shouted at the top of my lungs. "I want to see the hospital administrator, goddamnit."

Two nurses appeared out of a doorway. Down at the far end of the hall I could see a blonde, older woman coming our way.

"Jane," the woman called. She looked as tired and ragged as we did.

Jane turned to look through the blur of her tears. "Audrey?"

"It's all right, Jane," Audrey told her. "I've been with him since he collapsed at the studio. We've been trying to get hold of you. It took me a while to track you down."

"Is he—"

"He's better," she said. "We don't know yet how

bad it was, but the doctor thinks he'll come out of it all right. He was fine," she said, "fine just before the show. There wasn't any warning, just . . ."

She stopped. Jane held tightly to my arm.

"I want to see him," Jane said, quietly now.

"I'll show you the way. It's 2-417," Audrey said.

I hesitated.

"Come on, Keith. Stay with me," Jane asked. I think she needed me, maybe for the first time.

The witch at the desk piped up, "I'm sorry. Regulations say that—"

"Oh, shut up," Audrey told her. And the three of us walked down the hall.

When we reached Tom Flemming's room, Audrey opened the door and went in first. Jane hesitated, then tightened her grip on my hand and walked inside. Her mouth opened involuntarily as she saw her father.

Tom Flemming looked awful. His skin was gray and there were a dozen tubes and wires snaking to and from his body. These were connected to bottles, air tanks, and electronic gear at the side of the bed. The only sounds were the pulses and beeps of the apparatus, the awful hum of the machines, and the sick man's labored breathing.

"Can he . . . can he talk?" Jane asked.

"He's unconscious," Audrey said, "but stable now. The worst is over." They were whispering as if he were only asleep.

"The worst?"

"When he fell down at the mike, we thought . . ." Audrey stopped short and bit her lower lip.

"But he's going to be okay?" Jane asked.

"Yes."

"You're not just saying that."

"No, he's going to come through this," Audrey told her. The eyes of the two women met.

What neither of them said was what I knew—there would be damage. Nobody comes through a stroke with everything intact. But how much damage would there be? I looked at the Golden Voice of Radio, a tube in his mouth, a catheter clipped into his nose, and wondered if this was the end of his career.

Jane sat down on a chair next to the bed. Audrey asked if it would be all right for her to go home and get some rest. Jane nodded. We would stay through the night and Audrey would come back in the morning to see how things were. Morning seemed like a long time away.

After Audrey left I realized that my parents were probably wondering what had happened to me, so I left Jane at the bedside and called them. My father answered the phone. I told him how things stood and that I was staying at the hospital with Jane. He understood and said to call if he could help.

When I got back to the room I found Jane bent over the bed, her face pressed against her father's hand. Her eyes were closed and her cheeks were wet. I wondered if my coming in would disturb her, but I wanted to be with her. I knelt down beside Jane and took her hand. She squeezed mine.

"Keith?" She sat up.

"Yeah?"

"Do you believe in God? I mean, the real God."

"I don't know."

"Do you believe enough to pray? You used to go to church. Would you pray for my father?"

"Sure. So could you."

"God wouldn't listen to me. I'm too awful."

"No you're not."

"*I am,* Keith. Do you know, if he . . . if he doesn't make it, he'll think I hate him. He'll think I don't care."

"No he won't. Besides, he's going to be fine."

"But that's what I always told him, that I hated him. I was so busy getting even all the time that I made his life miserable. But Keith, he's all I've got." Jane was crying now. The tears fell down her cheeks like silent rain.

"It's all right, Jane." I tried to assure her.

"No it's not. Keith, pray for him. For me too. I want to change after all this. I really want to."

"All right."

"Now, Keith," Jane insisted.

I closed my eyes and prayed for Tom Flemming, for recovery, for Jane. I felt strange. I had not spoken to God like that since I was a kid.

"I'm scared," Jane said.

"I know."

"You know what's wrong with me, Keith?" Jane's voice was stronger now. "It's that I'm all twisted up in myself, all my lies and defenses and everything, so when I feel something I can't show how I feel because . . ."

"Yeah?"

"I think I'm too tired to figure out what I'm saying. Do you know what I mean?" She looked at me, her eyes rimmed in red.

"I think so. You're afraid to show how vulnerable

you are. That's why you have to get even all the time, because you're afraid of getting hurt. Just like everybody else."

"But I've got to stop, Keith. I can't keep on trying to get even with the whole world. I've got to learn to let the hurts go, or to handle them, somehow. Oh, I'm so screwed up."

"Take it easy on yourself, will you?"

"Keith," Jane said, "hold me."

I took her in my arms and she nestled her head against my shoulder. Even here, in this awful room, I felt myself wanting her.

"I really like you," she whispered to me.

"Oh," I answered. I don't know if I was disappointed or not, but she sensed it.

"I mean, I think I'm in love with you." She pressed her face into my shoulder after she spoke.

I reached up and held her face in my hands, then kissed her. It wasn't a frantic kiss like the ones back at the party. This one was slow, soft, and real.

"Did it hurt to say that?" I asked.

"No, but it wasn't easy."

"Are you glad you said it?" I wanted to hear more.

"Yeah." She smiled and then kissed me again.

Later we both slept a little. Jane sat beside the bed; I sat in a naugahyde armchair against the wall. Neither of us could really drop off, what with the nurses coming and going, but we were too tired to stay fully awake.

When the sun came up outside I got us some coffee from a machine to celebrate the new day. We watched the sky go from dull yellow to bright orange until, at last, the sun came up over the farmland east of the city. The morning light gave Jane her color back. Her skin was pink again and her hair glowed, honey blond and frizzy. She looked beautiful.

On the hospital bed, Mr. Flemming was stirring.

"Should we call a nurse?" I asked.

"Wait," Jane said. She watched her father as he pulled out of a deep sleep into some kind of half-waking. His eyes opened, still unseeing.

"Dad," Jane said. "Daddy."

He blinked and tried to move, but straps held him to the bed.

"Daddy, can you say something?"

A sound came out of his mouth, but if it was a word I couldn't recognize it.

Jane stroked her father's forehead with her hand. She wanted to say something too.

"Daddy."

He tried to answer her, air rushing past his lips but no sound coming with it. Then he tried again, but his tongue couldn't control the sound.

"Say it again," Jane told him.

Mr. Flemming marshaled his strength for another effort. At last it came out. "Euhh can tahh."

"What's he mean?" Jane asked me.

"I think he's saying, 'I can talk,' " I told her.

"That's right, Daddy, you can. You can talk. You're going to be fine as soon as they get all these tubes out of you. You're going to be just great."

He closed his eyes.

"Daddy," Jane said. "Don't go to sleep yet. I've got to tell you something."

Mr. Flemming blinked.

"Daddy," she said, her voice heavy with tears, "I love you. I really do love you."

Her father smiled as best he could. The smile told Jane what she had to know, that he heard, he understood. She would tell him again of her love, later when his strength returned. But this first time was the hardest.

Chapter 18

JANE

I'M WRITING THIS LAST CHAPTER WHILE KEITH IS breathing over my shoulder. He says he wants to see what I'm writing. More likely he's looking for an excuse to eat my earlobe.

Cut it out, Keith.

It's June, the end of the year at Wagnalls. Uncle John has become vice-principal, Mrs. Jennings has taken over his old job in guidance, and Mrs. Morris is rumored to be pregnant. Uncle John, on moving thirty feet to his new office, is reported to have mouthed some appropriate cliché like, "It's truly an honor and a privilege." Mrs. Jennings, also on the move, is rumored to have said, "I'll never fill his shoes." She was referring to the white ones. Lou Russell, shortly to be moving to the Harvard Quad, actually did say, "I didn't do it," referring, we think, to Mrs. Morris.

Not that any of this is very important. What *is*

important is harder to talk about. Let me try to get at it indirectly, by telling about dinner at our apartment last week. Maybe that will sum things up.

The dinner was a cozy little affair, as they say in the society columns, in which Mr. Thomas Flemming, his friend, Mrs. Audrey Beattie, and his charming daughter, Jane, entertained Mr. and Mrs. David Hartman and their son Keith. The party was to celebrate the recent recovery from illness of Mr. Flemming and his promotion to general manager of the local Barton Broadcasting affiliate. Mrs. Beattie wore a pink . . .

Oh, let me cut out the phoney postures. We had dinner, okay? I felt like wearing a dress, so I told Audrey, who immediately declared that it would be a dress-up dinner. The word was passed on to Keith, who wore his sport coat from Gordon's. Well, he tried.

My father put on a summer suit and combed the remnants of what had once been quite a head of hair so that he resembled a balding Cary Grant. The suit was a nice break from months of pajamas and bathrobes, and I had to admit that the old man looked good.

"And how do you feel now, Tom?" Keith's mother asked after the usual preliminaries were out of the way.

"Never better," my father boomed.

"You seem just fine," Mr. Hartman agreed.

"This n-new job of mine will have a lot l-less stress than the old one. My only real fear is that it might be too b-boring." My father's voice still rolled out like liquid thunder, but it had developed a slight stammer. It was the stammer which ended his days as a radio announcer and forced him to move upstairs. After the stroke I stopped calling him Golden Voice, not because it wasn't golden but because the memory would be cruel.

"Being general manager gives you a lot more power, I would think," Mrs. Hartman said.

"I suppose. But I spend most of my time shuffling paper," my father complained.

"It's about time you moved into management, Tom," Audrey piped in from the kitchen.

"But management means I have to be nice to people." My father laughed and the others joined him, but it was one of those half-funny, half-sad things to say. For a man who'd spent thirty years doing verbal assassinations over the air, it would be tough dealing with people in a nice way. I mean, *nice* wasn't a word you'd use to describe my father. Maybe opinionated or clever, but definitely not nice.

Of course this personality thing isn't the real problem with his new job. The real problem is that a station manager isn't a star. My father knew that in a year's time Tom Flemming, the Golden Voice of Radio, would be just a memory. People would no longer say, "So *you're* Tom Flemming," when he was introduced. He'd have to deal with "Sorry, I didn't catch the name." Tough stuff for my dad.

"Tom, have you ever thought about going into politics?" Keith's mother asked. I could see that this dinner would be more than just a social get-together. She was busy recruiting.

"I'm not sure I could compete with candidates of the quality you already have. Take that Pescatore fellow," my dad said with smiling sarcasm.

"Seriously."

"I am serious. When a b-buffoon like that gets elected mayor it makes all of us question the nature of politics."

"The only reason that Pescatore got elected was that no candidates of quality were willing to stand. Nobody is more aware of that than I am," Mrs. Hartman said with a sigh. "And it's one thing to shake your head and make fun of the man, but it's another to be willing to enter the political arena. A man like you, Tom, would make an excellent candidate. You know the issues, you're respected in the community, people trust you."

"Thanks very much, Liz, but . . ." my father said, backing off. He knows a corner when he's being pushed into one.

"You don't have to make any decisions now. The Federal race is a year off and I just think you should consider it," Mrs. Hartman continued.

"Liz," Mr. Hartman stepped in. "Maybe you could let the search committee work on its own time."

Audrey brought in a tray of appetizers from the kitchen and a bottle of champagne which was nicely chilled. My father gave the bottle a shake before uncorking it, which was dumb because a lot of champagne bubbled over onto the floor. What a waste!

"A toast," Audrey said, "to Tom's recovery and his new job." We drank to that.

"I'd like to propose a toast to Keith," my father said, "on being named editor of the yearbook."

And we drank to that. In fact, we went through a full bottle of champagne before dinner. We toasted, if I remember: Keith's upcoming show in Ann Arbor, the old yearbook, and recent developments in the study of nucleotides. That toast was from Keith's father, of course, and gave us all a good laugh. What on earth is a nucleotide?

"And I want to propose one last toast," my father said. "To Jane's trip to California."

"To the trip," Keith said, smiling.

Of course neither of them was really toasting the trip; they were celebrating the fact that I was finally going *somewhere* to see my mother. It had been almost five years, a long time. When Keith made me call to tell her about Dad's stroke, I wanted to die. I was shaking as I held the phone, and I cried when I hung up. But I had to do it, Keith said, and he was right. It was time to stop getting even with everybody, time to drop all the tough postures and stupid little routines I'd been using to hide from what I really felt. Of course, all that is easy enough to *say,* but it's harder to get it inside, especially when your skull is as thick as mine. What am I going to say to my mother when I step off the plane? How can I find something *genuine* to say after five years of phoney silence? I don't even want to think about it now, so let me get back to something I can handle. Like food.

After the champagne was finished, we sat down in the dining room to eat. Dinner was a mild shrimp curry put together by Audrey. It occurred to me while we were eating this gourmet entree that both my father and I were useless in the kitchen. At least after Audrey moved in with us there'd be some decent meals in the place. I might even have to diet. Imagine having to give up both cigarettes *and* food.

"You must have been surprised by the furor over the yearbook, Keith," Audrey said.

"Lou had to handle most of it," Keith told her.

"Imagine anybody thinking those pictures were obscene!" Mrs. Hartman came in. "It's that right-wing backlash we're seeing all over."

"The same mentality that gave us Pescatore," my dad said.

"The only thing that saved Lou," Keith went on, "was his acceptance to Harvard. They figured it would look bad if they tossed him out of Wagnalls before he graduated. The press would make too much of a stink."

"Not to mention the radio station," Audrey added.

"I think Uncle John was the only administrator on our side," Keith said. "The principal wanted to send the whole shipment back to Texas just to avoid trouble."

"It's incredible!" Keith's mother said, waxing indignant. "You'd think we were back in the fifties."

"The world is full of Piggies," I said.

"What's that?" she asked.

"Oh, nothing," I said. I didn't think it was worth the effort to explain the whole thing. Keith just smiled. He knew I was working hard to be nice to his mother. The day before, Keith had said he *expected* me to have a fight with her. Talk about smug! I vowed on the spot that I would have nothing but nice words to say to Mrs. Hartman. Nice words. However much I disliked her.

And I did. She's a very *pushy* woman. Unlike yours truly.

For dessert we had a cheesecake that Audrey and I had made the day before. It was scrumptious but I only let myself eat a single piece. I've been worrying about my weight lately. I even looked up anorexia nervosa to see if it could be artificially induced, but decided that a diet made more sense. I mean, I'm really *not* crazy.

"I understand your older boy was home for a while," Audrey said to Keith's mother.

"Yes, he came in just before exams, poor thing. A bit of a rough patch in his marriage," Mrs. Hartman answered.

Keith looked at me and I gave an exaggerated look at the ceiling. Mrs. Hartman's phrase "rough patch" was like using "bit of a drizzle" to describe a hurricane. In fact, Steven had come stumbling home in mid-April without wife, kid, bucks, or sanity. Keith called me up to say that his brother was suffering from a nervous breakdown but I explained that the correct term was depressive reaction. I don't think the terminology helped much.

"Steven's back in Ann Arbor now, so he can be closer to his daughter," Mrs. Hartman said.

"But Keith's show is still going ahead, isn't it?" Audrey asked. She knew that Sandra had arranged it all.

"No problems," Keith announced. "Sandra and I are still on good terms, and the gallery couldn't care less that I'm Steven Hartman's brother. They're just interested in me."

Keith's attitude about himself has really turned around in the past few months. After all the work I've done to build up his ego, I guess I should be glad to see him more self-confident. But sometimes I think I might have taken the whole project too far. All I wanted was a decent boyfriend, not a superstar. Keep that in mind, Keith, just in case your cortex starts swelling a little too much.

The older people were ready for liqueurs at this point, and that gave Keith and me a chance to sneak off to the kitchen on the pretense of making coffee.

"Hey, you look nice," he said.

"Stop trying to look down my dress," I teased.

"I can't help it."

"Of course you can help it. Now stop acting like a Piggie," I told him.

"Give me a break," Keith said. "I'm not really a Piggie and I'm not so much an Iggie any more either. So what's left?"

"Well, I don't know," I said, thinking about it for a second. "Let's just say that you're special."

"That's nice," he said, kissing me hard. He was pressing my back against the refrigerator as we made out.

"Hey, I thought you were making coffee out there," Audrey called from the dining room. There was some laughter from the others.

I broke away from Keith, grabbed the coffeepot, and went back to the dining room. Keith was right behind me. Both of us were embarrassed but, amazingly, the one who showed it was me!

"We were just looking out at the view," Keith explained.

"And the fog outside didn't interfere with that?" Audrey teased.

"Not at all," Keith said seriously enough. "Jane and

I have learned to see through the haze. All it takes is a little concentration."

The four of them laughed, assuming that Keith was just covering up what we were doing in the kitchen. But I knew better. I knew that what Keith said was the absolute truth.

"WELL, HAVING ME POSE AS A STUDENT was a good idea." Nancy stood up and reached for her canvas bag. "I'd like to get started. But first, I need to know if I have your permission to check things out my own way. I mean, I may have to break a few rules to get to the bottom of this."

"Whatever it takes. I'll clear it with the police," Mr. Parton said emphatically. "And don't go yet." He motioned for Nancy to sit again. "I may not be thinking too clearly these days, but I do know that you'll need a contact while you're here, somebody you can talk to freely. Someone who can introduce you to a lot of kids. The principal isn't going to help any student fit in. Even I know that."

"Your thinking's not all that fuzzy, Mr. Parton." Nancy laughed again. "So, who's my contact?"

"One of our seniors. A good student, completely trustworthy. And very popular, president of the class, which is why I chose him. He can get you in touch with all the various 'crowds.' "

"You mean he knows about me already?" Nancy asked.

"No, I thought I'd introduce you two and let him in on the plan at the same time." Mr. Parton checked his watch. "He should be here any minute."

At that moment, there was a knock at the door. Mr. Parton opened it, and Nancy looked up and found herself face to face with the beautiful driver of the black Porsche!

"Nancy Drew," the principal said, "meet Daryl Gray."

His eyes weren't brown or black, Nancy noticed immediately. They were the dark, dusky color of ripe blueberries, and they were rimmed with lashes that had to be at least half an inch long. Nancy had never seen eyes like that in her life.

Some contact! She thought.

Daryl Gray listened politely and with interest as Mr. Parton explained the entire situation. If he was surprised at Nancy's role, he didn't show it.

Instead, Daryl's incredible eyes kept straying to Nancy each time Mr. Parton mentioned her name. And when the principal said something about Daryl showing Nancy the ropes, Daryl's mouth curved into a slow, teasing grin. Nancy couldn't help returning it.

The attraction between them crackled like electricity. Nancy wondered how Mr. Parton could possibly miss the sparks, but he seemed oblivious to everything but his problem. He went on and on. As Nancy tuned out the principal's voice, she tuned into the beautiful face before her.

Finally the harried principal said something that brought Nancy back to reality. "Nancy, the school is counting on you. I've done what I can. Now it's up to you. At this moment, Daryl is the only one, aside from me, who knows who you are and what you're doing here. The rest is in your hands."

And Nancy, remembering that hideous voice on the tape, finally tore her eyes away from Daryl. *You're wrong, Mr. Parton,* she thought. *Somebody else knows who I am. And that's the person I have to find!*

The warning bell rang just as Nancy and Daryl left Mr. Parton's office. Together, they fell into step with the crowd of kids hurrying to their homeroom classes. Out of the corner of her eye, Nancy caught Daryl looking at her, a strange little smile on his lips. "What's funny?" she asked.

"Nothing." Daryl laughed softly and shook his head. "It's just that I've never met a detective, especially a beautiful redhead who drives a Mustang."

Nancy laughed too. "Well, I've never met a senior who drives a Porsche."

"It's my favorite toy," he replied. They rounded a corner and Daryl casually put his hand on Nancy's shoulder to guide her out of the way of a group of kids coming in the opposite direction. "I'll have to give you a ride sometime, show you what it can do."

At the touch of Daryl's hand, Nancy felt a delicious tingling sensation. Suddenly, she found herself wondering what it would be like to have Daryl's arms around her. Daryl Gray was a powerfully attractive guy.

"Do you think it would be good for making fast getaways?" Nancy went on in the same teasing manner.

"Sure," Daryl replied, leaving his hand

where it was, "but I hope you're not planning to make a getaway real soon. After all, we just met."

"And besides, I have a mystery to solve, remember?"

"Right. And I hope it takes a long, long time."

They were both laughing, looking into each other's eyes as they turned another corner and bumped into what felt to Nancy like a stone wall.

"Sorry," the wall said.

Nancy touched her nose to make sure it wasn't broken, and then smiled at the guy, who was big, handsome, and built like a truck.

"Wait, meet Nancy Drew. She's a transfer student," Daryl said smoothly. "Nancy, Walt Hogan."

Nancy smiled again, remembering what Bess had said about Bedford's football captain. "Hunk" fit him perfectly.

"Yeah," Walt said, not returning her smile, "nice to meet you."

Walt strode off, and Nancy turned to Daryl. "He seemed a little angry," she commented.

"Yeah, he hasn't been Mr. Friendly lately," Daryl agreed. "And you should see him in action, on the field. He's like a bear just out of hibernation—mean and hungry."

"I don't suppose he's a video freak, by any chance?"

"I thought detectives were supposed to be more subtle than that."

"Why should I be subtle with you?" Nancy teased. "You're my contact, aren't you?"

Daryl's hand tightened on Nancy's shoulder. "I sure am," he said softly.

Nancy and Daryl were standing in front of Nancy's homeroom class, waiting for the final bell to ring. About ten other kids were waiting, too, and as Nancy laughed at Daryl's last remark, she caught a girl staring at them.

The girl was blond, pretty in a tough, hard-edged kind of way, but she didn't look too friendly, Nancy thought. She was watching Daryl intently. Then as someone called out, "Carla!" the girl moved her eyes to Nancy's face for just a second before turning away. In that brief instant, she gave Nancy the strangest look. It wasn't a look of dislike, Nancy thought, it was more like a challenge. She wondered how much this Carla knew about her.

The final bell rang, and Daryl gave Nancy's shoulder another squeeze. "I guess this is it for now," he said. He leaned so close that Nancy felt his breath on her ear. "You're on your own, detective."

By the end of the next day, Nancy was ready to explode. First, Connie had treated her as if she had some horrible communicable disease. Then she couldn't find Walt Hogan or Hal Morgan so she hadn't been able to question them. Plus, her rear end still ached from that fall off the trampoline. Things were definitely not going well. What she wanted most of all was to go home and soak in a hot tub.

Instead, Nancy decided she'd better make another pass at the video lab. She didn't want to leave Bedford High empty-handed.

The lab wasn't locked. When Nancy walked in, the only person there was Daryl Gray, who was peering at a shelf of tapes. Suddenly, she felt happy for the first time all day.

"Am I glad to see you!" she cried.

Daryl spun around, startled. Then his lips parted in his Porsche-driver's grin. "Nancy Drew, isn't it? New girl and . . ." He glanced around at the otherwise empty room . . . "private eye? How's the detecting going?"

"Don't ask," Nancy said with a groan. "Anyway, what are you doing here? I didn't know you belonged to the video club."

"I don't," Daryl said. "I was just doing some detecting of my own—looking for you." He came to stand within hugging distance of Nancy. "Looks like we found each other."

The nearness of him made Nancy forget all her problems. "I'm glad we did," she said. "I'm so glad, in fact, that I'm inviting you to go for a Coke. Right now."

"Sounds great to me."

"Good. I'll drive," Nancy said teasingly, "and let you see what my Mustang can do."

As they walked through the parking lot, Nancy spotted Jake Webb among the cars. Probably siphoning gas, she thought. Every time she saw him she remembered how he'd threatened her on the stairs the day before. Was that his first threat? Or had he tried to scare her off before with the videotape?

Then Daryl put his hand casually on Nancy's shoulder and she forgot about Jake Webb and simply enjoyed the touch of Daryl Gray.

"How is it going, really?" Daryl asked

again as they got into the Mustang. "Have you found any clues? Are any of the pieces fitting together yet?"

Nancy started the car with a roar. "I never thought I'd say this," she admitted with a wry smile, "but right now, the last thing on earth I want to do is solve a mystery."

Glad to be leaving, Nancy headed out of the parking lot and down Bedford Road. Daryl didn't ask any more questions about the case, and she was grateful. There'd be plenty of time to think about it later. Just then, all she wanted to do was drive.

As they headed away from the high school, Bedford Road became narrow and winding. Through the trees, Nancy caught glimpses of water.

"That's Bedford Lake," Daryl pointed out. "It has some nice secluded benches. Why don't you drive down there?"

Down is right, Nancy thought, as the grade suddenly became steeper. She'd been doing about thirty-five, and all of a sudden the needle climbed to fifty. A blind curve was coming up. Nancy put her foot on the brake. The pedal sank to the floor, and her stomach sank with it.

"Hey," Daryl said, "I don't want to sound like a driver's ed teacher, but don't you think you should slow down a little?"

Nancy couldn't answer him. The brakes were gone, and her car was shooting down the winding road, completely out of control!

The car picked up speed, careening wildly down the hill. Nancy downshifted to second, then to first. The Mustang slowed, but not enough.

"Sharp curve coming up." Daryl spoke quietly, but Nancy heard the quaver in his voice. She couldn't blame him—she was too terrified to speak.

Hands glued to the wheel, Nancy guided the car into the curve, praying that she wouldn't meet another car coming up. The road remained clear, but it also grew steeper. And as she came out of the bend, she could see the stop sign at the bottom of the hill. It was still fifty yards away, but in her imagination she was already on top of it, could see the Mustang tearing into the intersection and colliding with whoever was unlucky enough to be in the wrong place at the wrong time.

Amazed that her hand was steady, Nancy reached over and slowly pulled up the handbrake. It didn't work. The stop sign was looming up like a monster's claw in a 3D movie. There was no time to think.

Instinctively, Nancy aimed her car at the soft shoulder on the opposite side of the road. With an impact that snapped their heads back, the Mustang hit the bank, went up on two wheels, and wobbled for what seemed like an eternity. But finally, with a bone-jarring thump, it landed upright.

Nancy shut her eyes and leaned her head on the steering wheel. She was breathing like a marathon runner. When she opened her eyes again, she saw Daryl pry his hand loose from the dashboard. "Well," he said with a gasp, "so that's what your Mustang can do."

Nancy reached for his hand and held on tight. She felt like crying, but when she opened her mouth, a giggle came out. It's a perfectly normal hysterical reaction, she told herself. Then she giggled again.

There was a smile in Daryl's voice as he said, "How about letting me in on the joke?"

"It's just . . ." Nancy tried to stop laughing and couldn't. ". . . I remembered that my car is due for an inspection in two weeks. Now the gears are probably stripped, the front bumper has to be completely smashed, and the brakes are burned out—" This last thought brought Nancy out of her dream world.

Her car! What had gone wrong? True, it needed an inspection, but that was just an official thing. Besides, she'd had new brakes installed six weeks ago. Something awfully strange was going on, and whatever it was, Nancy had a definite feeling that it wasn't good. She pushed open the door and jumped out.

"Hey! Where're you going?" Daryl called, rolling down his window. He stuck his head out and saw Nancy kneeling by the left front wheel, peering underneath the fender. "What is it?" he asked.

Nancy stood up, so angry she could hardly see straight. "The brake cable," she said grimly. "It's been cut."

"What?! Are you sure? I don't get it. Who'd . . .?"

"Wait!" Nancy held her hand up for quiet. Then she sniffed the air. Frowning, she ran to the back of the car and sniffed again.

"What's wrong now?"

Nancy could hardly believe what she was going to say. "That rock we went over—I think it cracked the gas tank. Daryl, the car could blow! It could blow any second!" She started down the hill. "Get out of the car. Hurry up!"

There were no footsteps behind her.

"Nancy!" she heard Daryl call. "Nancy, I can't open the door! It's jammed!"

Nancy didn't hesitate. She raced back to the car and fought with the door from the outside, but she couldn't get a good grip on the handle because the door was angled slightly toward her.

She ran to the driver's side. The smell of gas fumes was stronger than ever.

"Get your seat belt off," she said to Daryl as she finally managed to open her door. She helped him climb out. "Now let's *go!*" She grabbed his hand. "The car's already beginning to burn!" she said, as they ran desperately down the hill.

When the car blew, they were less than a dozen yards away from it. The force of the explosion flung them into the underbrush by the side of the road.

They clung to each other. For a moment, hardly able to speak, they stared at the burning sportscar.

"Nancy, are you all right?" Daryl whispered at last. His eyes were bright with concern.

Nancy nodded. Feeling the heat of Daryl's breath against her cheek, she hardly noticed her bruised knee and scratched arms. It seemed the most natural thing in the world for them to keep their arms around each other. Nancy closed her eyes and breathed deeply. When Daryl had first touched her two days before, she'd wondered what his arms would feel like. Now she knew—they felt fabulous.

But with that fabulous feeling came another feeling—guilt. It wasn't Ned whose arms were holding her; it wasn't Ned whose lips she was feeling, nor Ned whose voice was murmuring her name. And hadn't she said just three days before that nobody could compete with Ned Nickerson? Well, maybe no one could in the long run. But at the moment—in the short run—Daryl Gray was doing a pretty good job of it.

It was a dangerous moment, emotionally, and Nancy knew she wasn't ready to deal with it. Before Daryl's lips reached hers again, she eased herself gently from his arms.

"Hey," she said softly.

"Hey, yourself." Daryl's blue eyes were smiling. Looking at Nancy, he gave a long sigh. "So," he said, in a throaty voice, "how about answering the question I never got a chance to ask. "Who would do something crazy like this?"

"I have a pretty good idea." Anger made Nancy's voice tight. She pulled away and felt herself stiffen. "Does the name Jake Webb ring any bells?"

"Jake? Sure," Daryl said slowly, sitting up. "I can see him doing something like this. But there's no way you can prove it, is there?"

Don't Miss Your Chance To Be A Winner!

Fill in the entry blank provided below.

Name Telephone Number

Address State Zip

Age/Grade—Optional

1. No purchase necessary. To enter hand print your name, address, zip code, telephone number and age on the official entry form or on a 3 × 5 card. Mail the form to Simon & Schuster, Attn: ND FILES, 1230 Avenue of the Americas, New York, NY 10124-006. Entries must be received no later than 10/31/86. No photocopies allowed. One entry per envelope. No responsibility assumed for late, lost or misdirected mail.

2. All prizes will be awarded. Prizes are non-transferable and non-redeemable for cash. No substitutions allowed. One prize per person, address or household.

3. Winner will be randomly selected from all entries received.

4. Prizes are 2 Panasonic SG-X7 stereo systems—retail value of approximately $150.00 each, 50 Panasonic RX-4920 portable stereo radio cassette recorders—retail value of approximately $90.00 each, batteries not included, 200 Panasonic RF-433 compact AM/FM radios with headphones—retail value of approximately $26.00 each, batteries not included.

5. Prizes must be claimed within 30 days of notification attempt or prize is subject to forfeiture, in which case a substitute winner will be selected.

6. All taxes are the responsibility of the winners. Winners may be required to execute an affidavit for eligibility and release. Winners grant to Simon & Schuster the right to use their names and likenesses in advertising and promotion related to the sweepstakes.

7. The odds of winning will be determined by the number of entries received.

8. The sweepstakes is open to all residents of the U.S. except employees and their immediate families of Simon & Schuster and its agencies.

9. A list of major prize winners can be obtained by sending a self-addressed stamped envelope to: Winners List, c/o Simon & Schuster, THE NANCY DREW FILES SWEEPSTAKES, 1230 Avenue of the Americas, New York, NY 10124-006.

#2 CULT OF CRIME

The Hardys jet off on an all-expense paid trip to Paris, where their assignment is to investigate Paul Reynard, a French businessman who may just be the head of an international crime empire. Frank and Joe go undercover in Paris posing as punked-out drifters in search of illegal weapons. As soon as they arrive they are plunged into a nightmarish train of events, in which they are arrested, imprisoned, and framed as cop-killers. If they reveal their identities, they will blow their cover and alert Reynard. So they flee to Normandy, where, unknown to them the Reynard family has learned their mission and waits to execute them.

#3 EVIL, INC.

The Hardys set out to find Holly, a young girl who has fallen into the clutches of a California cult. The cult's background may be religious, but the motivation is pure crime. Frank and Joe manage to rescue Holly, but must flee cross country with both the police and angry cult members on their trail. What the Hardys don't realize is that Holly has been completely brainwashed. One word from the cult leader could set her off on a path of destruction so terrible that it could leave the town of Bayport in a state of total ruin.

Look for THE HARDY BOYS CASE FILES novels at your local bookstore!

Archway Paperbacks
Published by Pocket Books

NHB-2B